MARGARET BARLOW MYSTERIES

Murder
on the
Chesapeake

A MARGARET BARLOW MYSTERY

DAVID OSBORN

SIMON & SCHUSTER
NEW YORK LONDON TORONTO
SYDNEY TOKYO SINGAPORE

SIMON & SCHUSTER
Simon & Schuster Building
Rockefeller Center
1230 Avenue of the Americas
New York, New York 10020

SIMON & SCHUSTER and colophon are registered trademarks
of Simon & Schuster Inc.

Manufactured in the United States of America

10 9 8 7 6 5 4 3 2 1

Library of Congress Cataloging-in-Publication Data
Osborn, David
Murder on the Chesapeake/David Osborn.
p.   cm.
"A Margaret Barlow mystery."
I. Title.
PS3565.S37M84   1992

813'.54—dc20   92-2768
                                                  CIP

ISBN: 0-671-70486-9

To Margaret LaFarge Osborn

Prologue

AT 6:54 P.M. on the tenth of May, fourteen-year-old Mary Hughes, a scholarship student at Brides Hall, an exclusive girls' boarding school at Burnham on the Eastern Shore of Maryland, had only seven minutes before her life was, with premeditation, brutally extinguished by someone she trusted.

A forlorn and lonely child constantly burdened by the coldness or ridicule—depending on their whim—of her elitist schoolmates, she was seated at that precise moment in the freshman area of study hall in Main, a once-great antebellum plantation house, now the school's principal building.

Hunched over her lift-top desk, Mary glanced up at a big Roman-numeral clock and, seeing the time, felt a cold wave of fear rush through her body. Immersed in hated trigonometry, she had forgotten the chapel bell for vespers, which had to be rung at seven sharp. Freshmen always had the duty, taking it in turns, three days at a time. If more than a minute late at the onerous task, the culprit drew an additional two days of duty. Mary had been late five times in a row now, and the school buzzed and laughed at her clumsiness and misfortune.

The chapel was some distance away, and Mary knew she would only get to it in time if nothing happened to delay her. Six fifty-five. A minute lost already. Trigonometry with all its inexplicable angles, its functions and endless degrees, would have to wait its further torture of her tired mind until after bedtime. Then, hoping every minute not to be discovered by the ogress dorm monitor in one of her slipper-silent forays from room to room, Mary would wait until her three roommates were huddled sleeping lumps in their iron bedsteads before going under the covers herself with the trigonometry text and flashlight, to try desperately once more to fathom and to remember.

Rising from her desk and careful not to let her chair scrape too loudly on the wide-planked floor worn by successive generations of students, Mary tucked the book under her light-blue cardigan, pressing it flat under her arm so it could not be seen. Books were not allowed to be taken from study hall by freshmen. Each student's texts had to be kept neatly stowed in her assigned desk, and the study-hall monitor, always a privileged senior, usually random-checked by lifting the lid of a desk here and there, and putting on report any girl who broke the rule. At Brides Hall, violators seldom escaped the punishment of extra study hours on Sunday.

The monitor that night was at the supervisory desk at the far end of the room as Mary walked up the aisle dividing the freshmen from the sophomores, for whom study hall was also mandatory, and from those juniors who were required to attend because of flagging grades. There were sideways glances as she passed and relieved realization that her requesting permission to leave meant the hated study period was nearly over for everyone.

At Brides Hall freshmen don't speak to a senior unless spoken to, and the previous night the monitor on duty had made Mary wait before recognizing her presence; first just for form's sake to emphasize her authority and then deliberately even longer to make her late in ringing the bells.

This night, however, Mary felt a wave of relief. The senior was one who was usually kind.

"Yes, Mary?"

"Please, ma'am. Permission to ring the bells for vespers."

And then the misery of the wait, even though a short one. The clock showed Mary she now had but four minutes.

Would she be asked if she was stealing out a book? Please don't let her ask. Please.

The senior's cool unwavering brown eyes beneath the straight dark hair, held back neatly with an expensive gold-and-tortoiseshell barrette, for a moment gave nothing.

"Do you have the key?"

"Yes, ma'am."

Mary felt its hard irregular shape in the pocket of her cardigan where she'd put it after taking it from the office key rack just before study. The tall young body at the desk leaned languidly; a pencil tentatively tapped the smooth surface of the desktop.

"Permission granted, Mary." A smile, a flicker of sympathy. "And don't goof it, okay? Tonight is your last time if you don't."

"Yes, ma'am."

As Mary turned quickly to leave, the cool voice came again, the smile still in it. "And walk, Mary. Don't run."

"Yes, ma'am."

A snicker from someone close by. A snapped "silence" from the senior, the smile gone instantly from her face.

And Mary's heart pounding in her ears as she walked as fast as she dared back down the aisle between the desks, the forbidden trigonometry book hugged to her ribs. Her thin body rigid with anxiety, she pushed through swinging doors into the silent carpeted width of Main's spacious hallway. Its great double stairway swept upward majestically to the library and school infirmary above and on up another flight to the Repository and attic storerooms.

Mary did not run, since freshmen weren't allowed to run anywhere at any time except during athletics. She quickly descended the worn limestone steps that led from Main's wide, columned portico onto the graveled path which in turn wound around the back of the building to the large grassy, elm-shaded quadrangle, one side of which was dominated by the old chapel.

Easter had come and gone and with it a three-week vacation. School had resumed with spring settled in full over the Eastern Shore and summer rapidly approaching. Magnolia, wild cherry and dogwood were in full blossom, and along roadsides, trumpet creeper in brilliant orange flower and tree-size holly were in full leaf. Woods and field were rapidly greening, and in marshy places the din of tree frogs joined the song of migrating birds. The rich smell of earth's renewal was in the soft evening air. The sun had just set, and the sky was beginning to deepen into soft mauves and purples, heralding twilight and first stars.

The weathered gray stone of the old chapel was covered with ivy, refreshed now after the winter, and a breath of early night air, coming up Burnham Creek from the Little Choptank River and Chesapeake Bay beyond, rustled the leaves into a faint whisper of sound. School tradition had it that the chapel was haunted; once a black slave woman had been murdered there, every girl knew, her throat cut by a jealous husband as she knelt before the altar praying for her lover killed in a Civil War battle. Weren't those dark stains on the flagstone floor her blood?

Mary felt a sharp stab of superstitious fear as she fitted her key to the heavy oak door. And then surprise when she found the door already unlocked. It was her job, too, to lock up after vespers and return the key to the office. Had she forgotten last night? If so, surely her error would have been discovered by now, by a cleaner or a security guard, and she would have been reported.

She had no reason to know that the person who had opened the door was waiting for her in the darkness within.

There was a complaining creak of hinges as the door swung open and, immediately, the familiar musty smell of the chapel's interior, the damp of old prayer books and pew cushions and the dank of old plaster.

She groped for the light switch just to the right of the door. The dim glow from the two inadequate chandeliers threw grotesque shadows everywhere.

The chapel was not large. Originally it had doubled as a Congregational meetinghouse, and a balcony with a double row of pews, under stained-glass windows, surrounded three sides. Below, a dozen more pews each side of a center aisle helped to seat most of the Brides Hall student body of three hundred and fifty. There were vespers every evening for the first three classes. Seniors were excused from chapel except for Sunday service, when attendance was required by the entire student body as well as by most of the thirty-odd faculty.

Mary moved quickly now. How much time was left? Half a minute? Less? With no one to see her, she ran for the door to the narrow stair leading to the balcony, threw it open and dashed upward as fast as she could.

Reaching the top, she rushed along the narrow balcony toward the choir and where the two quarter-inch bell ropes, dangling through a hole in the ceiling and knotted near their ends to make pulling easier, were looped fast around a wooden cleat fixed onto the wall. She had just tossed her textbook onto the seat of a pew and was freeing the ropes when her murderer was revealed.

"Hurry, Mary. You don't want to be late again, do you?"

The unexpected voice, shattering the silence, caught Mary completely by surprise. A scream rose in her throat, then died when she turned and recognized who had spoken.

Mary managed a relieved smile and shook her head. Confident of her safety, she braced herself to pull the ropes. Behind her, the murderer moved fast. In one sure motion, the dangling loose end of one rope was scooped up and flipped around Mary's neck and tied rapidly into a lethal loop. With a knee thrust savagely into Mary's back, the looped was pulled and twisted death-tight.

Strangling doesn't take long. A moment of utter surprise, of agonizing pain; terror next with hands scrabbling at the rope, then animal panic as lungs desperately seek air. All to no avail. A terrible inner head roar and onrushing darkness.

When Mary's body sagged, her murderer looped the rope

around her neck again, threw a disguising coil around her body, picked up the frail little figure and threw it off the balcony.

A violent jerk. The rope held.

High above, the bell clanged once. Hard.

In the study hall, students heard it and rushed to put away books. Nobody questioned why the bell had only rung once. Mary was a "reject," someone who didn't fit into school society and never would. It was just the sort of thing she'd do, ring the bell just once.

Some laughed. Mary would have bell duty once again.

They were wrong.

{1}

I FIRST HEARD ABOUT Mary the morning after it happened. Some of the tragedy, anyway. The full truth didn't come out until much later. My daughter, Johanna, called me from the midtown Manhattan office where she is a partner in a corporate law firm occupying the top three floors of a forty-story glass tower.

"Mom?"

"I'm here," I answered groggily. The bedroom curtains were drawn, shutting out the morning light from my Manhattan East Side apartment, along with some of New York's endless uproar. I focused with difficulty on the little Swiss traveling clock on my bedside table. It was just after eight.

I immediately thought she was calling about Christopher or Nancy, my grandchildren. "What's happened?" I asked.

"I'm not quite sure. I got a call from Ellen Mornay just before I left for the office . . . No, nothing's happened to Nancy. Mornay says she's fine, just upset."

For a lawyer, my daughter could be remarkably non-specific, and I fought down a wave of exasperation. "Upset about what, Johanna?"

"Well, there's been some kind of terrible accident at school."

And then silence.

I exploded. "For God's sake, what kind of an accident? What are you talking about?"

"The chapel balcony. A girl fell off it and hanged herself. One of the freshmen."

The two words instantly shocked me. "Hanged herself?"

"With one of the bell ropes."

I did some hurried remembering. The only time the chapel bell was rung except for Sunday service was for vespers at seven in the evening right after study hall and right before dinner. "When? Last night?"

"Yes. Apparently she went to ring the bell for vespers and got tangled up somehow and fell. You know how those ropes are."

I certainly did. Like my daughter and now Nancy, I'd once rung them often enough.

"Mornay said the girl was friendly with Nancy. Mary somebody or other."

"Mary Hughes?"

"Something like that. Yes, Hughes. I haven't talked to Nancy yet so I'm not positive, but I think that's it."

Nancy had mentioned a Mary Hughes in several of her letters, said she was a scholarship student from a poor family and that everyone always picked on her.

I think I had known all along what my daughter was going to ask. I think I realized it the moment she mentioned Brides Hall. Over the years I have developed an acute premonitionary sense about her calls. I'm a free-lance photojournalist and I was due Saturday morning to photograph a weekend glider contest near Front Royal, Virginia, at the foot of the Blue Ridge Mountains, and also to participate, as gliding is a hobby of mine. Today was Thursday and I'd planned to drive down Friday morning. Brides Hall was more or less on the way, which Johanna knew.

"Since you were heading in that direction anyway, I just wondered if you wouldn't want to stop and check on Nancy"

"I can go down today, I suppose, if you think it's urgent," I said. "I can spend the night at school and go on to Virginia on Friday."

"Oh, Mom, could you?"—knowing full well I'd say yes, of course I could.

After we hung up, I stayed in bed a few minutes, feeling

conned and not quite certain if I minded or not. My daughter, whom I love very much, bless her, has never quite decided, as I suppose many modern women have not, which is more important in her life, her children or her work. Unlike me, she doesn't need to work; her husband, also a lawyer, earns enough to provide anything any reasonable woman could ever want. But she likes work; work is food and drink and air to her, so she had long ago found the ideal solution to her dilemma. Me. In a classic piece of feminine logic, she decided that as long as her children were with me, she felt they were with her. Thus I take Christopher, aged eleven, and Nancy, thirteen, with me every summer to Martha's Vineyard and the lovely old eighteenth-century house at Edgartown George and I shared during nearly twenty-five years of happy marriage and which he left me when he died eleven years ago. I also fill in whenever my daughter and her husband manage to coordinate their frequent business trips away from the frenzy and clutter of New York City. Friends say that along with my work, this keeps me youthful, and I guess it does. I admit, reluctantly, to being in my mid-fifties. Judging from the male attention I've received over the years, and my grandchildren's delight in spending time with me, I believe I pass for younger, physically and otherwise. Jane Fonda aerobics and an every-other-day two-mile run help to keep me in good-enough shape to cope with two energetic kids.

After my aerobics workout I showered, dried my hair and decided it needed a touch more highlighting to offset the several new streaks of gray creeping into the natural blond. Then I camouflaged some objectionable minicrow's-feet around my eyes with carefully applied eye makeup, dabbed on some of my favorite perfume and got ready to pack. I never use lipstick.

Normally, I'm a balloonist, but a year ago someone persuaded me to take up gliding. I did and I love it. I've already logged quite a number of hours, although I'm not sure if I don't still find ballooning more of a "trip." Certainly, if you're taking aerial photographs, it's far easier to shoot from the relatively roomy stability of a balloon's gondola than from the cramped confines of a sailplane's cockpit.

I have a once bright, now faded, yellow zip-up nylon jumpsuit with a mess of useful pockets which I wear for both forms of aerial escape. I packed that first, stuffing it, along with oxygen mask, helmet, gloves, binoculars and a six-foot pure-silk white scarf, last year's Christmas present from Johanna, into a nylon carryall.

Next, I loaded my camera bag with my two cameras, extra lenses and filters, and film, got out my most respectable suitcase and packed for Brides Hall. No doubt there would be dinner with Ellen Mornay, the Headmistress, along with some of her staff. It could still be cool in the evening on the Eastern Shore, so I decided on a rather smartly tailored light gabardine suit. I added a denim skirt and a striped cashmere sweater-dress with belts suitable for both, and selected several practical blouses, a light cardigan and a classic blazer for walking about the campus. Then I dressed for the trip: tailored flannel slacks, a blouse and sweater and a well-worn pair of penny moccasins I always wear when driving.

Half an hour later I went down the street to the garage and got my old station wagon, and I was on my way. The car clock said ten-thirty. I estimated I would be at Burnham, Maryland, and Brides Hall, between three and four o'clock, giving myself a half hour to stop someplace for coffee and a sandwich.

I was of two minds as I drove. I was concerned for Nancy; the death of a friend at any age is difficult but especially so in adolescence when one usually does not have the experience or maturity to understand and cope with grief. I was also thoroughly uncomfortable at the thought of visiting Brides Hall, perhaps with good reason.

Brides Hall is the reigning queen, and has been for a very long time, of America's all-girl preparatory boarding schools, whether East or West. Scholastically, athletically and socially, it is number one. Several daughters of American Presidents have gone there, as well as daughters of some of Europe's leading statesmen. Titles are scattered throughout its alumnae lists. For years its graduates were automatically accepted into any Ivy League college of their choice.

But I have only been back to Brides Hall three times in all the years since I went there myself. The first time was when I took my daughter there. The last was this fall, when Nancy entered her freshman year. For some odd nostalgia I have never been able to explain, even to myself, I paid the school a visit one alumnae weekend fifteen years ago.

Why have my visits been so rare? The answer is simple. My years there were mostly unhappy ones. I went to Brides Hall, like Mary Hughes, on a scholarship and found myself in a world essentially composed of a kind of elitism and social snobbery with which I was unprepared to cope. When it was discovered that my father did not belong to the Social Register or the Blue Book, nor to any *Who's Who* of industry, banking and other favored "establishment" turf, I was quickly labeled a "reject," and if not outwardly snubbed, then simply ignored. Hurt and angry, I wanted to leave at the end of my first term and only stayed to please my father; it seemed to mean so much to him. "Stick with it, Margaret," he said. "You're getting the best education in America." When that categorical statement slowly dawned on me as being true, I stayed voluntarily right to the end.

The years were tough. This was no old-fashioned "finishing school," although originally founded as such in 1868 by Miss Meredithe Taylor—Meredithe with an *e*, mind you. She had been a Baltimore spinster who felt an urgent need to educate marriageable young ladies of class in the niceties of running the refined home they would unquestionably one day be mistress of, along with the rarefied social life that would go with it. Time had changed all that. Upon her death in 1876, her more ambitious assistant, one Ethel Worthington Cadbury, a secret feminist who had with iron self-discipline held her tongue on her opinions about education, expanded Brides Hall in a matter of a few years into a proper educational facility. As subsequent headmistresses came and went, physics, biology, mathematics, chemistry, English literature and foreign languages crept in. I don't think I ever had less than four hours of homework every day and on weekends invariably more than ten. And I never in any year carried less than five subjects at a time.

Brides Hall students also were expected to go out for sports, and I made captain of the tennis team; they had to give me that when I won the school tournament two years running and in my senior year the interschool tournament. I graduated cum laude and was politely applauded when I received the honor prize for history. Would I have done it again knowing all I did when I left? Yes, perhaps. But when my daughter insisted on following in my footsteps, I protested. In vain, obviously. And I protested again when she decided to send Nancy. Nancy is a different sort of girl from either her mother or grandmother. She's far more of a dreamer, less determined. True, she wasn't at Brides Hall on a scholarship as I was, and her parents weren't an unimportant family from a small town in western Nebraska. Johanna and her husband "belonged." Just the same, I agonized over what I thought Nancy would suffer because she *was* so sensitive. For quite different reasons she didn't belong at Brides Hall any more than I had. And now, it seemed, I had fresh cause to worry about her.

It was, however, the most beautiful of spring days. The Delaware countryside was lovely in its warm, fresh green mantle, and I was nothing but optimistic. No matter how upset Nancy might be, I was certain I would be able to help her. Equally, I was quite unable to conceive that my old alma mater would be anything less than welcoming regardless of my personal feelings about it.

{2}

THE EASTERN SHORE of Maryland is the name given to what is actually the Delmarva Peninsula, a one-hundred-and-fifty-mile-long, low-lying coastal plain bounded on the west by Chesapeake Bay and on the east first fronting relatively sheltered Delaware Bay, then shouldering the open Atlantic Ocean. Beginning not far from Pennsylvania, it ends far south in a slender, windswept sandbar tail at Cape Charles in Virginia, fifteen miles across the mouth of the Chesapeake from Cape Henry and the great naval base at Norfolk.

Where the Western side of Chesapeake seems busy with the port of Baltimore and the huge yacht conglomerates around Annapolis and the U.S. Naval College, as well as with the important influxes of the Susquehanna, Patuxent and Potomac rivers, the Eastern Shore, in contrast, still almost gives the sense of stepping back a century. In spite of a myriad of marinas and harbors sheltering fishing fleets and yachts alike, there is a backwater beauty, a sleepy timelessness about much of it, as though once leisurely plantation life still influenced the very air, whose soft scent of forest and field is always touched with a breath of the sea, and where towns with names such as Oxford, Royal Oak, Queenstown and Sherwood evoke images of early English settlers.

By afternoon, I'd finally got far down the peninsula and was headed westward through Dorchester County toward the Chesapeake. Driving through a landscape of pine and

19

oak woodlands that broke a vast flat panorama of corn and soybean fields, I felt myself slowly drawn into another world. The narrowing rural road itself was not unlike one of the many meandering creeks and small rivers that made slow, almost dreamlike progress toward Chesapeake Bay. There they ended in a profile of narrow bays and shallow muddy tidal estuaries that created a thousand-mile coastline as jagged as a torn piece of muslin, and where life was the sea and no longer farming.

I bypassed the town of Cambridge and took a country road that swung down the bay-indented south side of the Little Choptank River toward Taylors Island, a Chesapeake Bay promontory some ten or twelve miles distant. I passed historic old Trinity Church, built in 1670, then, a little farther on, the villages of Woolford and Madison, and suddenly I was in Burnham.

Overlooking Burnham Creek, a tributary of the Little Choptank, Burnham is the smallest of places. A church, the Dorchester National Bank, Meritt's grocery, Owen's feed and grain store, Enos Brandt's tackle shop and the Burnham Inn, a pub with a few guest rooms dating back to 1740, cluster around the shallow rectangle of the village green with its traditional Civil War cannon and pyramid of cannonballs. All brick or wooden buildings, they form a solid encircling wall of long-established and unhurried stability broken only by a main road that connects Burnham with the rest of the world.

It was two-thirty in the afternoon. With a quickening sense of expectancy akin to stage fright, I drove slowly around the green, seeing almost no one except two state troopers standing by a cruiser drawn up in front of the bank. I thought their presence a little odd. How odd, I was to discover almost at once, when one of them, a man with premature jowls and paunch and a low-slung revolver holster, heard the rattle of my station wagon and turned sharply to put his hand out for me to stop. Since he also stepped into my path, I had little choice. When I braked, he came around to my side of the car and asked to see my driver's license and registration.

I was too surprised to speak. Obviously he hadn't seen me do anything wrong, since his back had been turned to me until I was less than a hundred feet from him.

"Where are you headed, Margaret?"

That did it. Partly because I've never been one to have much liking for police and can't stand first-name familiarity by complete strangers, but mostly because of my nervousness at going back to Brides Hall, I was unable to control my instant irritation.

"If you mean *Mrs.* Barlow," I snapped, "since we haven't yet been introduced, Brides Hall."

He stiffened visibly, retreated, and silently handed me back my papers. "It's that road there," he said, pointing to a narrow lane that began just ahead at the side of the Burnham Inn.

"And I was probably driving it before you were born, officer," I said. I put my wagon in gear, stepped on the gas and, I guess, came close to running over his feet as I shot forward. In my rearview mirror, as I took the lane out of the square, I saw him, hands on hips, staring after me. If body language means anything, he wasn't very happy.

Slowly getting myself in hand, I drove perhaps a half mile on the narrow blacktop, avoiding the occasional pothole and wondering why, if the county couldn't afford to repair the road or couldn't get around to it, the trustees of Brides Hall didn't. The school hardly lacked funds; its endowment was over forty million dollars. And then, all of a sudden, there was that familiar long avenue of pasture oaks, imported as seedlings from England well over two hundred years ago, their hoary trunks half-buried in deep hedges of tuja which crowded in on the road.

The oaks ended, the road bent sharply before a large sign saying SLOW, and there they were, the huge, ornate, wrought-iron gates attached to massive granite pillars which announced the school. Beyond them, a tailored gravel drive swept past open playing fields to end at Main, the finest of mid-eighteenth-century residences on which, over time, various wings had been built. Before the Civil War and Miss Meredithe Taylor's subsequent arrival, Main, with its classic colonnaded front porch, had been the center of a five-thousand-acre cattle- and slave-breeding farm known as Drummers. Little distinction, if any, as I understand it, was ever made between the two highly profitable activities run for five generations by the Compton family, notable in Maryland politics for their furious defense of states' rights until the collapse of the Confederacy put an end to their hegemony.

Main was the only one of the farm's many buildings used by Miss Taylor, since its spacious, high-ceilinged rooms were more than adequate for the twenty-five young ladies she instructed in the gentle arts of refined manners. Under the succeeding Miss Cadbury and subsequent headmistresses, restoration of some other buildings had begun until, by World War I, every original plantation building still standing was in use and new ones had been built besides.

I drove through the gates. Halfway up the drive I could see to my right, across the playing fields, the two raked masts and high bowsprits of *The Maryland Queen* tied up at a wharf in sleepy, narrow Burnham Creek, next to the two boat houses which sheltered the school's many canoes, rowboats and windsurfer boards. A replica of a famous early 1800s Chesapeake Bay packet schooner, the sixty-foot gaff-staysail-rigged *Queen* was presented to the school by a wealthy Chicago alumna in 1926 to replace a far too small sloop, a Chesapeake Bay skipjack oyster dragger. It was now used to teach the girls sailing, and its shorter, stubbier, single mast could also be seen as it rode at anchor out on Burnham Creek itself.

As I approached Main, the outlying buildings behind it appeared. There were a dozen of them, large and small, clustered around an elm-shaded quadrangle. Closest to me and the driveway was the familiar outline of the fateful chapel, the only building made of stone. Three lower brick buildings across the quadrangle, formerly "harem" quarters for the scores of young female slaves continually breeding, were now dormitories. Five others at the quadrangle's far end, once barns and stables, had become the school's principal classrooms and a gymnasium.

Beyond all this, I glimpsed the low modern stable built for those students fortunate enough to own a horse and who wanted to keep it at school. Down a flower-banked path was the Smoke House. About twelve years ago, Ellen Mornay had it converted into six guest suites, each suitably decorated to cater to the tastes of wealthy parents who wished to spend more than a few hours at school when visiting a daughter.

A word about Ellen here. She and I had been at Brides Hall together, she a year ahead of me and the girl most responsible for much of the social ridicule aimed at me. Her father was a prominent Boston Brahmin, but during my junior year he became involved, to my secret delight, in some sort of career-ruining insider scandal.

I disliked Ellen intensely, but I grudgingly admired her for what she'd accomplished at the school. Twenty-five years ago, when she first took over, Brides Hall had been on a serious downward slide. Its academic standing had dropped badly, staff morale was at rock bottom. It had begun to attract fewer and fewer students from prestigious families, and even the school grounds and buildings were beginning to look shabby. After college Ellen had chosen education as her career and was at that time Assistant Headmistress at a prominent prep school outside Boston. She was approached by the trustees of Brides Hall, who were desperate to turn things around and who felt that someone familiar with the place might be their best hope.

Their choice had not been proved wrong. With great energy, devotion and intelligence, Ellen had not only put the school back on its feet physically and morally, making it number one among all its prep school peers, she'd also tirelessly worked to build up its dwindling endowment to the more than comfrotable sum it was now. In doing all this, she had made her name famous in private education. Running Brides Hall was now universally considered an open door to a deanship in almost any prestigious university, to most educators the final exalted reward. Only this past Saturday, I'd read in the *New York Times*, Ellen had made the gala-dinner keynote address to eight hundred other preparatory school executives at their annual National Association for Private Education convention in New York's Waldorf-Astoria hotel. NAPE members, the *Times* said, had given her a standing ovation.

As I reflected on this, the driveway widened into a large oval for turning and parking. I pulled up next to a powder-blue Alfa Romeo sports convertible and got out. For a moment, I just stood there collecting my thoughts, unprepared as always for the most breathtaking beauty of Main's architecture and for its size. It was a big three-storied white building of nearly perfect proportions, a paean to everyone's idea of the classic Southern plantation house.

I must have been like that, just staring, for over a minute when I suddenly realized my name was being called.

"Margaret! Margaret!"

I looked up to see Ellen Mornay herself coming down the front steps toward me.

{3}

I'D MISSED ELLEN when I brought Nancy down to school in the fall and hadn't seen her since the alumnae weekend fifteen years previous. If I can be forgiven a certain secret vindictive pleasure, in view of the enmity between us as schoolgirls, I had been amused then to see time had not been nearly as kind to her as it had been to me.

In spite of the important public-relations aspect of her job, Ellen had become a classically drab schoolmarm. Her makeup was either nonexistent or all the wrong kind, her clothes were dowdy, her straight dark hair styled by someone totally uninspired, and her overweight body soft and lumpy.

Expecting her to be even less attractive now, imagine my surprise at seeing the slender, smartly dressed woman who approached briskly and with the warmest possible smile took my hands and brushed her cheek against mine. I almost didn't recognize her. It was her voice, always a little too loud and calculating for my liking, that told me who she was; her voice and a small but distinctive mole high on her left cheek.

"Margaret, it's so good to see you. How are you and how was the trip down?"

"I'm fine, Ellen, thank you. And the trip was mostly the usual ugly New Jersey. Why they named it the Garden State I'll never know."

She laughed. "Johanna called this morning and I had

25

Gertie Abrams send a maid down to Suite One right away. You are spending the night, aren't you?"

"If it's all right. I know you must have your hands full."

"Of course it's all right. Nancy will be thrilled."

Two senior girls came out of Main and Ellen called them over.

"Margaret, this is Constance Burgess. Constance, this is Mrs. Barlow, an alumna of Brides Hall. She took those lovely pictures of the Alps we all saw in *Life* magazine last year."

I found myself looking into an extraordinarily beautiful face and the bluest eyes imaginable beneath nearly platinum blond hair. I knew right away who she was. Nancy had mentioned her in letters. She was the only daughter of Texas billionaire Hiram Burgess, and this year's Head Girl, a position of authority as well as prestige to which she had been elected by the girls themselves. In spite of her youth, which I judged was probably eighteen, she had a stunning, fully mature figure and an air of sophistication one would expect to find in a college senior, not a high school girl.

We shook hands, Constance welcoming me with a noticeable Texas accent. Then Ellen said, "And this is Cynthia Brown. Sissy is captain of the *Queen* this year."

I took an immediate and instinctive aversion to the second girl. Nearly six feet tall and with the broad muscular shoulders of an oarsman, she had short brunette hair, cut like a boy's, challenging and slightly mocking eyes that were a little too close together, and a bone-crusher handshake. There was a self-confident aggression about her and an almost rebelliously strong sexuality that suggested to me she's already been around with many men. I also marked her down at once as a bully who would take advantage of her size, strength and seniority and, what I was certain were her considerable athletic abilities, to terrorize underclassmen generally.

I made what I hoped were appropriate noises of appreciation for her being the *Queen*'s skipper, something of great importance at Brides Hall, and then Ellen said, "Constance, would you mind taking Mrs. Barlow's bags down to Suite One directly. Gertie's had the maids make it ready and the door should be open."

"Of course, Miss Mornay."

The Head Girl took my suitcase and carryall from the back seat of the station wagon and handed them to Sissy Brown, who hefted both as though they were feathers, then the two girls promptly headed directly across the grass of the quadrangle in the direction of the old Smoke House. Only seniors were allowed to walk on the grass; everyone else had to use the encircling gravel path. As I watched them go, I wondered why the school didn't run a road down to the guest suites—many parents must have come there with far more baggage than I—and as though reading my mind, Ellen Mornay said, "I recently proposed a road to the Smoke House but the trustees turned it down, saying we had plenty of students to carry bags. The swing vote came from John Ratygen, of all people. I could happily have killed him. You remember John, don't you?"

I did. Now he was the senior Senator from California and Chairman of the Senate Armed Services Committee, a highly publicized and controversial Washington figure in the process of a rather nasty divorce from a wife of many years. In my day at Brides Hall he'd been a student at St. Hubert's, a leading boys' prep school at Chesterton not too far away and captain of the school's football team. Ellen had had quite a crush on him.

I said that I did remember John but didn't know he was a school trustee.

Ellen laughed and told me he'd been one for some time, and then, apparently satisfied I was impressed with her having such a famous personage on the school's board of trustees, dropped Ratygen and said quite abruptly, "We've had lunch, Margaret, but I can ask the kitchen to fix something for you and bring it to my office."

I thanked her and said I'd stopped for a sandwich on the way down. I suddenly had a feeling of being hemmed in, especially when she went right on. "Then perhaps you'd just like to freshen up before you see Nancy. I think she's in special study hall right now. She's been having trouble with French. I'll have her brought to my office."

Crisp. Efficient. Bossy. An order to me to come to her office. Why on earth should I? And why would she want me and Nancy there? I couldn't believe she was just being hospitable. I wanted to say I'd just as soon have Nancy join me in the guest suite where we could be alone, but instead found myself politely surrendering and hating myself for doing so. I agreed to be there in fifteen minutes. Then, with the uncomfortable feeling of again being a student, which had grown on me ever since I arrived, I dutifully headed toward the Smoke House.

In our brief meeting, neither Ellen nor I had mentioned why I was there. Indeed, we had both carefully avoided the subject. That was natural, I thought. The accidental demise of a student in a boarding school is nearly akin to disaster. There'd be plenty of time, I knew, to offer my sympathies and to find out exactly what had happened.

I stopped a moment as I began to cross the quadrangle. I was close to the chapel where the tragedy had occurred. The vestry door was open and the musty odor of the chapel's interior drifted out to me. I didn't know then, of course, how Mary Hughes had actually met her death, but standing there looking at the old ivy-covered walls of the chapel, I had a strange feeling—I really can't say what it was—a sense of something horrible, of true evil, really, that in spite of the warmth of the day made me shiver. Shiver and want to run, not just from the chapel but from Brides Hall itself. The feeling was so strong I think I would have retrieved my luggage and driven away at once without any explanation or apology if it had not been for Nancy.

I was about to continue on when I was startled by the sudden appearance in the vestry doorway of a man I at once presumed was a teacher. I guessed him to be in his early to mid-forties and he was, to put it plainly, incredibly handsome, not in the conventional macho sense but rather in the sensitivity of his wide mouth and deep-set eyes, and in the almost catlike stance of his perhaps too lean body. He was relatively dark-skinned, possibly Italian or Greek in heritage. He wore running shoes, jeans, a T-shirt, a windbreaker zipped only halfway up, and he had an unruly mop of dark hair. I guess I must have been staring because he suddenly smiled and pointed in the direction of the Smoke House. "The girls went that way, Mrs. Barlow." He had a soft but firm voice.

"I know," I said. I wondered how he knew my name.

He looked me up and down slowly but not rudely and then smiled again, his eyes quietly amused. "Enjoy your stay," he said. And disappeared back into the gloom of the old chapel as silently as he had appeared.

For some reason, I felt rather indignant, as though some sort of protective wall I'd automatically raised around myself the moment I'd arrived had been breached. What did he teach? I wondered. Gym immediately sprang to mind. It always does at a girls' school where a man is concerned, especially an attractive one. It's hard to imagine a math or history teacher having sex appeal. One thinks immediately of tennis or soccer or something akin to them. Except something about this man didn't fit any kind of jock image. Too much intelligence in his eyes, I thought, too much sensitivity and, at the same time, too much chained energy behind the quiet exterior.

{4}

THE OLD SMOKE HOUSE was a two-storied brick building nestled against a darkly thicketed wood some hundred yards distant from the stables beyond the quadrangle. It was the far side of the loveliest of flower gardens through which I passed on a flagstone path that wove between deep borders of super elfins and blue ageratum. Behind, some of the forthcoming summer's lupines, delphiniums, hollyhocks and foxgloves were beginning to show signs of blooming.

There were three guest suites on the first floor, three on the second. My room was to be Suite One, on the first floor.

It had been done up for millionaire couples, with two bedrooms, a living room, and a kitchenette. The decor was a combination of expensive English country and French provincial with lovely floral-pattern chintz curtains to match William Morris wallpaper. The bathroom was wall-to-wall, floor-to-ceiling Italian marble with brass fixtures; it had an oversized Jacuzzi, a bidet and a double stall shower and double sinks. The kitchenette had sculpted oak cupboard doors, an electric stove, a microwave oven and a full-size freezer/refrigerator which I found stocked with every imaginable type of liquor, along with bar snacks. And there was a coffee machine that certainly put mine to shame. Mine made regular coffee. And very nicely, thank you. This one did too, and also made espresso or cappuccino.

By the time I walked in, the two senior girls had stowed my suitcase on a smart baggage rack, opened curtains and windows, letting in the daylight and fresh air, and had turned down a bed in one of the bedrooms. They showed me everything there for my convenience: the television, VCR, tape library, the stereo, telephone, et cetera, then started to retreat. I don't know what got into me; curiosity finally overcame my good judgment, I suppose. I stopped them at the door and asked about the accident, and the result was slightly embarrassing for me. Their response was not reticence, as I had expected. It was pure evasion.

Both girls instantly became guarded, especially Sissy Brown. Constance Burgess was the one who answered my question. "You'll excuse us, Mrs. Barlow, but Miss Mornay has asked us not to discuss the accident with anyone. I'm sure she'll be able to tell you anything you want to know."

And that was that. Smiles. Direct eye contact, perfect courtesy. And no information.

I said I understood. What else could I do? I quickly looked for something to say to cover the slightly awkward silence that followed. I remembered that parents' weekend was coming up. I asked the usual mundane question, were they looking forward to it. And got the usual mundane answer, "yes." And then, also knowing that parents' weekend was the occasion of the annual twenty-four-hour Chesapeake Bay race between *The Maryland Queen* and *The Chesapeake*, a sister-ship packet-boat replica owned by St. Hubert's, I made polite noises to Sissy Brown, expressing my certainty that her Brides Hall crew would carry away the cup this year.

The girls left. I changed into my suit and low-heeled suede shoes and then headed back for Main.

As I recrossed the quadrangle and walked past the chapel, I glanced again at the open vestry door, I suppose to catch a glimpse of the man I'd seen before. He wasn't to be seen, however, and I didn't linger.

Ellen Mornay's study, along with all other administrative offices, was on the ground floor of Main beyond the study hall, with a supervisory view over the quadrangle at classrooms, gymnasium and dormitories, as well as the old chapel. It was the sort of place you'd expect the study of the Headmistress of a very expensive school to be, suitably businesslike and femininely luxurious at the same time. There were chairs and a couch and a low cocktail table on brass legs; a beautiful English leather-topped desk, muted draperies, prints on the walls, along with photos of *The Maryland Queen* in action as well as various past school photos of Mornay's and my days there.

I paid no attention to any of this at the moment, however. My thoughts were on the young girl who leapt to her feet when I entered and flung her arms around my neck.

"Margaret!"

I was struck immediately by how pale and drawn Nancy looked, but I said nothing to that effect, deciding to wait until Nancy and I could be alone.

Sitting there in Mornay's office, with Nancy silent and tensely expectant beside me, and with Mornay being more suspiciously relaxed and charming than I ever could have thought possible, doors in my mind unlocked and I found almost to my surprise that I still knew the school ways inside and out, its traditions and its rules and how things were or were not done.

We spoke at first of such trivia as Nancy's progress in school and my forthcoming glider event as well as my usual summer plans to take Nancy and her brother to Martha's Vineyard. I congratulated Ellen on her speech Saturday to NAPE in New York. She expressed appreciation of an article about me as a balloonist which had appeared in a magazine. I saw her wince once or twice when Nancy called me "Margaret," but I was not about to explain that being called "Grandma" didn't really fit in with my plan not to become geriatric until the last possible moment. Nancy and her brother were under strict orders never to address me by anything but my first name.

All this nonsense eventually came to an end, and we finally got to the purpose of my visit: Mary Hughes.

Hanging is hardly a pretty end to a life. Ellen and I both avoided any details of Mary's death except for Ellen's explaining how Mary had gone into the chapel to ring the bells for vespers and for some reason must have stood up on the balcony rail while holding the bell ropes and then had become entangled somehow and fallen. One of the seniors, assigned that week to open the chapel's main doors and take a head count on entering students, had discovered the tragedy and was treated for shock by an ambulance crew.

I learned that Mary came from Norfolk, Virginia, from a lower-income family, her father being a chief petty officer in the Navy.

"She hadn't been doing all that well," Ellen confided, "either in her studies or where interaction with other students was concerned."

I felt Nancy stiffen beside me when she said that. I couldn't see her expression, but if it changed, Ellen didn't seem to notice. Or perhaps simply did not care. She went right on. "But things were beginning to improve." She gestured that fate, which clearly put an end to that improvement, was something nobody could control; it was just one of those things in life.

Nancy, to her credit, remained stone-silent, staring down at her interlaced fingers.

We were suddenly bordering on unpleasantness. Ellen would have to have been aware of the parallel between Mary Hughes and me as a schoolgirl, and I could see in her eyes that indeed she was. I, too, had had difficulty with my studies my first two years; private elementary schools are usually far ahead of public schools where the scholastic basics needed to survive in prep school are concerned, and almost the entire student body except for me had enjoyed the best elementary education money could buy.

And I, too, Lord knows, had experienced difficulty "interacting" with other students. And indeed, why not? Being snubbed and ridiculed and called a "reject" because your parents "don't belong" would make it difficult for anyone, let alone a teenager, to interact with another person.

I kept my face expressionless, however, and Ellen, who had been my worst tormentor, looked relieved.

Eventually, it was all over. Ellen was hurrying off to a staff meeting with my promise to sit at her table in the dining room that night. Nancy was excused from sport, in her case lacrosse, to spend the rest of the afternoon with me. We left Main with no particular plan. Nancy was unusually quiet, though. I decided to wait until she told me herself what was troubling her—I sensed it was more than just Mary's death. We started idly across the playing fields toward the school's boat houses and *The Maryland Queen*, secure at its wharf.

Girls were already streaming out onto the playing fields, energetic figures in their blue sports uniforms: pleated skirts, blue knee-length socks and white blouses; some in body mature women, some virtually still children. Their calls and shouts, the clash of hockey and lacrosse sticks, stirred memories I wanted to forget.

We'd almost reached our destination when Nancy suddenly broke her silence with a low cry. "Margaret." She stopped dead, staring blindly at the slow-moving, muddy water of Burnham Creek. Her face was twisted, her eyes brimming with tears.

Whatever she'd been holding back was finally too much to contain. I drew her close. "Darling, what is it?"

"Margaret, Mary didn't die by accident. She committed suicide and everyone in school knows it. Especially that old witch Mornay."

{5}

"IT WAS BECAUSE OF Dead Monkey," Nancy went on bitterly. "Everyone knows that. Mary got him this year. Vicki Alcott willed him to her because she was assigned to be Mary's mentor. And Saturday, when Vicki came by and wanted to see him, and Mary went to take him down, he was gone."

I looked into her pale, tear-strained face and tried to make sense of what she was saying. "Take him down from where, Nancy?" I asked.

"From behind her suitcase on the top shelf of her closet," Nancy said. "That's where she put Dead Monkey the very first day she had him because she was so scared something might happen to him. And Vicki said she'd lost him and the seniors held an Inquisition and it was all so unfair."

We'd boarded *The Maryland Queen,* and I sat Nancy down on a hatch cover, put my arm around her and let her cry herself out for a while.

Across Burnham Creek, the woods coming down to the water were vivid lime-green, with only the occasional dogwood or wild cherry in flower to remind one of the final passage of spring. Above, the sky was blue-blue-blue and cloudless, and the sun was warm on us. From time to time the boat would rock almost imperceptibly in an eddy of current or from a slight waft of wind coming up the creek from the Little Choptank River and the Chesapeake Bay beyond. Far in the distance from a marsh someplace, I heard migrating ducks calling out in chorus.

All that is reality, I thought, *and what Nancy is telling me is not. What Nancy is telling me is a sick dream I have always tried to forget.* But my memory took me back over the years to a pathetic little terrified fourteen-year-old, confessing before a circle of jeering, laughing seniors holding an Inquisition her most intimate secrets as she kneeled. That, too, had been because of Dead Monkey.

Every school has traditions. Brides Hall has far too many, to my way of thinking. Some to me were archaic, meaningless in the modern world, even when it signified preserving a continuity with the past or teaching elementary self-discipline. Others I thought were vicious and destructive.

One of these was the tradition built up around Dead Monkey, a stuffed toy animal the size of an eight-year-old and worn hairless by time. Nobody knows where the great ugly thing came from originally or how it even got its rather nasty name. One day back in 1889, it was simply there and was passed on by its now unknown senior owner at Christmastime to the freshman to whom she'd been assigned as mentor, along with a loving good-luck message on a plain baggage tag pinned to its chest. It never left the school after that, nor was it allowed to. The freshman, three years later when a senior herself, "willed" it in turn to the freshman to whom she was now mentor and the "inheritance" continued from then on so that every three years the awful creature had a new guardian.

At Christmastime, there had also developed an embellishment to the tradition, with everyone at school sending Dead Monkey a Christmas card inscribed with a jingle or limerick of some sort. The Head Girl judged which one was the best and it was pinned up on the school bulletin board in Main for a month, then was put away in Dead Monkey's "locker" with the "inheritance" tags. This was a large metal box kept in the school library on the second floor of Main. The key for it was tucked away in a pocket in Dead Monkey's back, perhaps originally meant for a girl's or boy's nightdress. Down through the years, Dead Monkey's clothes had partially echoed the times the girls lived in. They were always male, and these days, according to Nancy, it was dressed in jeans, a blue-and-white rugby shirt matching the school's sports colors, and a battered yellow hard hat.

All seemingly innocent except for one thing. Tradition also held guardianship of Dead Monkey to be a sacred duty involving the honor of the entire school. Loss or damage to the creature by its guardian earned her disgrace and peer punishment. Brought before a secret gathering of seniors, the current guardian was stripped naked to her underpants and frequently even of them, and besides being harangued with the most personal questions imaginable, she was made to race around on her hands and knees, bark like a dog and sit up and beg for the dubious pleasure of eating a slice of raw liver.

A sensitive fourteen-year-old, perhaps never before away from home and probably half terrified of the all-powerful seniors, who would have seemed grown women to her, could be psychologically scarred for life by such an experience, but nobody seemed to care about that. As a senior, I had attended one such Inquisition and had been sickened by it. Afterward I had earned the enmity of half the school by revealing what had gone on and by openly crusading, and failing, to have the tradition abolished.

"Mary didn't lose Dead Monkey, Margaret," Nancy now said. "But nobody would believe her." Her tears had finally dried and her stricken expression had changed to one of stubborn anger. "Somebody stole it, that's what happened. When she was out of her room. Everybody knows that. The whole school. And they were all laughing at her. They were so mean you couldn't believe it."

I felt a long-forgotten step of pain, remembering only too well how it felt. I knew, too, that the seniors probably hadn't worried about possibly irate parents where Mary was concerned. The fathers of full-scholarship students

weren't likely to complain about their daughters being mis-
treated, so Mary's Inquisition would have been made to
last longer than most.

"Sissy Brown was absolutely horrible to her," Nancy
said. "I mean really cruel, because Sissy left her carryall in
the gym one day and Mary found it and turned it in to the
office. Mary didn't know who it belonged to and she didn't
want to be nosy and look inside. I would have done the
same thing. But the people in the office looked and found
some pot. It was only just a little bit, but Sissy got suspended
for two months."

The Inquisition had obviously been a day of vengeance
for the captain of *The Maryland Queen*.

"When it was all over," Nancy went on, "Mary cried
and cried and the liver made her sick and she threw up all
night. And she told me the next day she was going to run
away and maybe even kill herself. I guess except for Gertie,
I was the only friend she had."

I asked Nancy about Gertie. That was Gertrude Abrams,
the school housekeeper. She'd been a young first-year maid
in my senior year, a plain, rather sour girl who I always
suspected as bitterly envious of the more fortunate girls she
had to clean up after.

"I think Gertie felt sorry for her," Nancy explained. "She
used to invite Mary up to her room and give her cookies
and cocoa."

Identifying with someone she saw as unfortunate as herself,
I thought as Nancy and I left the *Queen* and headed back
over the now emptying playing fields. It was study-hall
time and here and there a last few girls hurried for the gym
locker rooms to change out of sports clothes.

"I bet Sissy stole Dead Monkey, Margaret," my granddaughter said. "Just to get Mary in trouble."

I agreed with Nancy that such could have been the case
but told her she'd probably never be able to prove it. "It's
one of those horrid things in life, Nancy, that you simply
have to live with while you get on with everything else."

"You won't say I told you anything, Margaret?"

"Of course not, dear."

"I mean, the seniors would really give it to me if they ever thought I'd told you what I did."

I saw her off at study hall and went back to the guest suite, had a drink, watched the evening news on television, dressed for dinner and then, feeling rather apprehensive, went back up to Main.

The dining room, along with its attendant kitchen, was in a one-story, low-ceilinged and unobtrusive wing of Main facing the school's front gates. It was built in 1904 to house classrooms that subsequently had been moved across the quadrangle to the former extensive stables. Approached by a service drive branching off from the main driveway and mostly hidden by a high thick hedge of hawthorn, it didn't mar the magnificent lines of Main itself.

Dinner was cafeteria-style, served by a kitchen staff of six. Various teachers presided over some thirty round tables each seating some ten or twelve students. At Ellen's and as a visiting "parent," I was deferred to by one and all with scrupulous politeness.

For my benefit, I suppose, Ellen had replaced the students at her table that week with several staff members and a few select seniors, including the Head Girl, Constance Burgess, and Gale Saunders, a stunningly lovely, amber-eyed, soft-spoken brunette from Philadelphia who was first mate and principal navigator of *The Maryland Queen* and who, I later learned, was the girl who had discovered Mary Hughes hanging from the chapel balcony.

I found myself seated between Onslow Weekes, the athletic director and head coach, and Arthur Purcell, the school's comptroller, a narrow-bodied man of about fifty with a weak cruelty about his mouth and in his pale narrow eyes, which darted expressionless behind rimless glasses, rarely fixing on the person to whom he was speaking.

Weekes was a young man I would have classified as a "pretty boy" with a rather high opinion of himself, especially of his biceps and pectorals, carefully cultivated, no doubt, by endless weightlifting to impress the girls. He was relatively short, the sort of coach who strutted a gym rather than walked it. I'd heard he had a young wife and two children under the age of three, yet twice I caught him clearly appraising Gale Saunders as well as Constance Burgess, not as students, but as women and potential bedmates. I couldn't help but wonder why Ellen had asked him to join us, unless to have him brief me thoroughly on the chances *The Maryland Queen* had of winning that year's race against St. Hubert's *The Chesapeake*. It was Weekes's last year as the crew's coach and supervisory captain, a policy decision having been made, after objections to a "mixed crew" were filed by St. Hubert's, not to have any male on board in the future.

Most of the time I found myself talking across him to Theresa Carr, the diminutive, strongly feminist Assistant Headmistress, whom the school affectionately called Terri. I later learned she had been instrumental in getting herself on board the *Queen* as co-coach for this year's race and then replacing Weekes completely next year and thereafter, something that had made him highly resentful toward her.

Terri was an earnest, pretty young woman in her late twenties who, Ellen Mornay told me, was invaluable in her virtually encyclopedic knowledge of every student. They, in turn, all clearly adored her, and I'd liked her myself the moment we'd met when I'd brought Nancy to school in the fall.

Terri had been born to a family of modest means and had risen up the educational ladder by hard work and competence. She told me with a guileless frankness I hadn't got from Ellen that they had real problems with some of the girls, who became quite hysterical the night of the "accident," one even spreading the word that Mary had been murdered by a lunatic escaped from a state asylum.

"But I think we've got them all pretty much under control now, Mrs. Barlow," she said. There'd been laughter in her eyes as she spoke, and I had the feeling she enjoyed a greater rapport with adolescent minds and emotions than did Ellen.

There was a kind of controlled half-hush in the dining hall, the usual clamor three hundred and fifty girls make all talking at once noticeably absent. Clearly Ellen Mornay's "no talking about the accident" order had been highly effective. I knew it wasn't just to keep the girls in order: parents' weekends was in two weeks. Mornay would not want any evidence of overwrought emotions and borderline hysteria, with all the attendant dramatic exaggeration inimitable to adolescence. An equal order had gone out to the staff, especially where the press was concerned. A curious local reporter, along with a more aggressive colleague from Washington, had been unceremoniously shown the front gates by Curtiss, the veteran chief of the school's five-man security force.

I was in a rather subdued mood myself. I talked, I smiled, I made polite conversation. I listened with false appreciation to Ellen telling me about the big new $26-million all-weather sports and entertainment complex which had been donated to the school by Hiram Burgess and for which ground was to be broken by Burgess himself that coming autumn. The complex would include a gymnasium, a swimming pool, a hockey rink, squash courts, three indoor tennis courts and a large film, lecture and theater auditorium that would seat eight hundred. It was indeed an extraordinary gift from which thousands of Brides Hall girls would benefit for years to come.

My thoughts, however, were on Nancy and everything she had told me. If the hateful tradition of the Inquisition turned out to have indeed caused Mary to kill herself, by law there would have to be a coroner's inquest. Girls, Nancy among them, were certain to be questioned. I didn't think Ellen would dare ask them, especially Nancy, with me now in the picture, to keep their thoughts to themselves, and if a coroner did decide Mary was a suicide, the school would be in a most uncomfortable position where parents were concerned. Some, certainly, would be sure to wonder what conditions existed here that could drive a poor child of fourteen to take her own life. And if the school was blameless as to the cause, they would have to wonder, too, why someone could not have seen the child was deeply depressed and arranged for professional help.

I left dinner that evening feeling disturbed as well as depressed. I didn't like seeing my dear Nancy upset. I went to her room to say good night and listened once more to her telling me how unhappy Mary had been and how unfair the Inquisition was and how she hated Sissy Brown.

I spent nearly an hour with her, and it was suddenly lights-out. I offered to have her spend the night with me in the guest suite, but she refused. "I'm not afraid of ghosts, Margaret. If Mary came back here to the dormitory, I wouldn't be frightened of her."

I had to leave quite early in the morning and wouldn't see her again, so we kissed good-bye with my promise to call her when I got back to New York.

Nancy might not worry about ghosts, and I suppose I didn't either, really, but passing the chapel on my walk back to the guest suite, I shivered involuntarily. The dim outline of the chapel and the now darkened school buildings, the long shadows created by the old-fashioned street lamps widely spaced around the quadrangle and on the path to the stables and old Smoke House, the whisper of night air through the branches of the quadrangle's huge elms, all slightly spooked me—to use an old-fashioned expression. I got quite a start, then, when I realized the lights of the guest suite were on—surely I had turned them off?

I received an even greater fright after entering the suite. I heard someone moving about in the bedroom and then that someone suddenly turned off the light there and appeared in the bedroom doorway.

"Good evening, Mrs. Barlow."

I recognized her at once, even though I had not seen her since I'd left Brides Hall for college. The same bony shoulders and arms, the same ungainly, work-worn hands, the hollow chest, the wispy hair—now quite gray—pulled back from a narrow face and held in a tight bun above the nape of a ligament-knotted neck; the same sour, hostile expression and thin, sexless, tight lips. It was Gertrude Abrams, the housekeeper. I offered her my best smile and warmest tone. "Gertrude, how awfully nice to see you again. How are you?"

She hardly rose to the occasion. Perhaps she heard the falseness in my tone. Her expression remained as unfriendly as ever and she didn't return my greeting. "I came down to make sure the maids prepared the suite correctly," she said in her rather brittle tone.

I said I'd found everything perfect. Indeed, someone had opened my suitcase and taken out my nightgown and laid it carefully on the turned-down bed and put my old Swiss traveling clock on the bedside table. It crossed my mind that she might have come to the suite for some other purpose, but I couldn't think what.

Her reply to my approval was curt. "Very well, madam. I'll say good night, then."

I followed her to the front door to show her out. I confess to being slightly cowed and made a last effort. "Gertrude, Nancy tells me you were close to poor Mary. I'm so dreadfully sorry for what happened. You must feel very bad about it."

She turned, stared at me and snapped, "I wasn't no closer to her than nobody around here. I don't know where Nancy got that from."

I waited as she disappeared rapidly into the darkness of the campus. I went back inside, undressed and took a shower, careful first to pull down all the blinds and draw the curtains, particularly those on the wooded side of the suite where the night beyond the windows was a solid wall of impenetrable black.

While the hot water flowed over my body, rinsing away a luxurious lather of marvelously scented and very expensive French soap provided in the suite, I tried to get my mind off Brides Hall and onto the gliding I would be doing

Saturday. But I kept coming back to the school and its problems, and later, in bed, when I'd turned off the light, I found myself reliving scenes of my own student days I'd long chosen to forget. Eventually I fell asleep, but not before verbally, in my imagination, berating my daughter for insisting Nancy go to Brides Hall. I could hardly wait for morning when I'd be able to leave the place.

{6}

ESCAPE PROVED IMPOSSIBLE. On Saturday, even at seventeen thousand feet over Virginia, the lovely countryside below, a patchwork of green and brown farmland giving way in the west to the deeper green woods of the Blue Ridge Mountains, I was still immersed in my old alma mater. Behind the rhythmical and sonorous sound of my own breathing through the rubbery face clamp of the oxygen mask I had put on at twelve thousand feet, I kept hearing the sound of hundreds of girls in the dining hall, their cries on the playing fields, and Nancy's strangled statement, "Margaret, Mary didn't die by accident. She committed suicide and everyone at school knows it."

I was in a single-seat, German-built fiberglass sailplane weighing slightly less than five hundred pounds, with a wingspan of about forty-five feet. It was a lovely, responsive little thing, although a bulky backpack parachute made it cramped in the cockpit, and as warm as a greenhouse with the sun's heat trapped by a bubble canopy.

The contest was to gain winning altitude within two hours of tow-off. The time of day allotted to each pilot had been determined by draw. There were fourteen of us in the Class-C event, and we were towed off at ten-minute intervals, beginning at 11 A.M. I had drawn seventh slot, which meant I left the ground at noon, a good hour to catch best what were by then rapidly building midday ther-

45

mals: rising columns of warm air caused by the sun's heat-
ing the earth and by which a glider pilot, feeling his way
like a soaring bird, is borne upward.

When I threw the cable-release lever detaching me at
five hundred feet from the tow plane, I was alone and in
wonderful silence except for a whisper of air moving over
my two wings cantilevered just behind the cockpit. I caught
a strong thermal almost immediately. It was several
hundred yards in diameter and rose over three thousand
feet before it dissipated. I found another and climbed up
to nearly nine thousand and then soared gently into the
slightly lesser strength of a third, which took me in slow
circles up to about twelve.

It was a good day for gliding, almost perfect, but my lack
of concentration cost me a win, and some pictures I took
weren't much good, either. I missed one giant thermal with
a diameter of at least five hundred yards which would have
surely carried me up to over twenty-one thousand feet.
This was the winning altitude achieved by a lively and
delightful young Vietnamese woman, once a boat person,
who had been in the same student class as I in Elmira, New
York, and with whom I occasionally went ballooning, most
recently over the Canadian Rockies.

We had such a good time that the winner and I agreed
to meet again the following Saturday, when we could have
a second, unofficial, contest. It would be a good excuse to
come down and see Nancy again.

I spent the night in Washington having dinner with old
friends. I rose relatively early, in good spirits, having managed to exorcise Brides Hall and Mary Hughes from my
thoughts.

I wasn't to be allowed to reprieve for long, however. I
had hardly reached the hotel's cashier to pay my bill when
I became aware of someone rising from a lobby chair and
coming toward me.

"Good morning, Mrs. Barlow."

I stopped, confronted by the vaguely familiar face of the

man I had seen just a few days before, smiling at me from the vestry door of the chapel at Brides Hall. I was completely taken off-guard, and I must have just stared in open-faced surprise. But yes, it was him all right: the same eyes, the same unruly mop of dark hair, the same lean, catlike body now dressed in a dark, well-tailored business suit with a white shirt and quiet tie. I guessed his age to be probably in his mid-forties.

Then I got the same slow smile I'd received the first time I saw him, and I heard him say, "Lieutenant Michael Dominic, Homicide Division, Maryland State Police."

He had his wallet ready and flipped it open. The ID card, large enough for me to read easily, had his photo, and a state police badge was pinned onto the wallet's opposite side.

"My apologies for breaking in on your day like this, Mrs. Barlow, especially so early. I did try to call your room just now, but you must have already been on the way down. I wonder if I could prevail on you to have a cup of coffee with me."

I finally found my voice and said, rather inanely when I think of it now, "Officially?"

His smile faded slightly. "Unfortunately, yes. I'd like to talk to you about Mary Hughes."

He'd hardly finished saying her name when I thought, Oh, my God, this man is a police officer, so Nancy must be right. "The accident," I said. And stared at him, waiting. Did I realize there was worse to come? I may have. I may have read something in his eyes because I felt a sudden tightness in my chest, and I knew that it was fear.

"Accident, yes. That's what it's been called," he said. "But I'm afraid it's a bit more serious than that."

And then I knew—call it intuition if you wish—but I knew. And tried desperately not to, so I fenced.

"You think it's suicide, too."

"No," he replied slowly. The smile had disappeared completely now, and his eyes had taken on a strangely hard quality. "No, we don't think it's suicide. Or an accident. We're pretty certain it was murder."

And there it was. I don't remember a lot for the next few minutes. Except wondering how he knew who I was, how he'd found me and what he might want from me. Before I could really even organize those questions, let alone ask them or speculate on the answers, I found myself seated in the coffee shop. After he ordered coffee, I asked him how they knew it was murder.

"Medical report," he said. "She was dead before she went off the balcony."

"Oh, my God," I said. "For how long?"

"A minute. Less. She was strangled with the bell rope. It was deliberately tangled around her neck and then she was thrown off."

My face must have revealed the shock I felt, horror, really, because he said gently, "I'm sorry, but we're sure of it. That's what happened."

I got control of myself enough to say, "You've told Ellen Mornay, of course."

"Of course. Yesterday, the moment we received the final pathology report and were absolutely certain. We met with her and Miss Carr."

"What do they plan to do? Close the school? Have they told the students?"

"No to both questions." He laughed wryly. "With us around, I'm sure the girls will soon figure out on their own what's happened, and Mornay and Carr were both adamant about carrying on just as they are, so the school stays open. Mornay planned to talk to the trustees, but she was certain they'd agree. The idea is to minimize the whole situation. I'm inclined to think that's right."

"You don't think the girls are in any danger?"

"Not immediately, no." He told me that the police were positive the murder had not been committed by some intruding maniac. Curtiss or someone on his security staff would have spotted any stranger on the campus, they thought. Besides that, the autopsy had shown no sign of sexual abuse, nor had Mary been beaten, both likely if she'd been killed by an outsider. Similarly, he explained, she obviously had not interrupted a robbery; there was nothing to steal in the chapel. Nor had she been robbed herself. And it seemed also unlikely, he said, that Mary could have been killed because she had interrupted something going on in the chapel which should not have been going on. He was certain the murder was premeditated and equally sure it had been done by someone at Brides Hall.

That made sense to me, but with the initial shock of his announcement over, I began to think clearly and now wondered about Nancy. Since she had been close to Mary, she might know something, even innocently, that could worry a killer.

I told him this. "My granddaughter was almost Mary's only friend," I added.

"We know that," he said, "but we don't think she's in any immediate danger either. We're keeping a close eye on her, just the same. I have plainclothes people on the campus, and she's never out of their sight for one minute. Would you want her sent home?"

"I'm not sure," I replied. And I wasn't. I knew it would upset her profoundly to be the only one taken out of school. Besides that, sending her home could also permanently fix the whole incident in her mind as something unresolved and perhaps terrify her, with the realization that she might have been in jeopardy as well.

"What about her parents?" he asked.

I told him that they would probably be pretty much guided by my judgment. And then I finally got around to asking him what he wanted from me and how he'd found me.

"The school told me where you'd gone," he said. A hint of impatience had crept into his voice. He clearly had no use for explaining anything he did. "The gliding event has been well publicized. Police in Front Royal found someone who'd heard you'd be stopping off in Washington. We tried all the hotels."

"But why?" I insisted.

Again that smile, as though apologizing for being a little short with me. "I also did some homework," he said. "When I learned your name before you arrived at the school Thursday and then heard your granddaughter had told some of her friends that you were involved in a multiple murder case on Martha's Vineyard, I called the police there and verified it. They said you were very helpful."

That whole awful summer rushed back to me then, and I could have killed Nancy on the spot for having mentioned Martha's Vineyard, especially when I'd made her promise me not to. I had gotten involved all right, becoming an amateur sleuth, as it turned out, and helping to solve the whole grisly mess. But I wanted the incident put behind me.

I must have looked the way I felt, for Lieutenant Dominic said apologetically, "They also told me the murders were particularly nasty, so I'm sorry if I've brought back unpleasant memories."

"You have," I said. "Now do please, Lieutenant, come to the point. What do you want from me? Information about the school? I'm afraid there's very little I can tell you. I've had almost nothing to do with the place since I graduated. And staying there overnight I heard and saw nothing which could possibly be of any use to you."

"No," he agreed, "I don't suppose you did. But you might if you went back there and stayed a week or ten days."

I guess, in retrospect, I knew that's what was coming. My immediate reaction was to leap up and run. Lieutenant Dominic was a good-looking and charming man, but he was still a police officer, and I wanted nothing ever again to do with any police investigation of any crime, especially murder. I scooped up my shoulder bag and half pushed my chair back. "I'm sorry, Lieutenant, but that's absolutely out of the question."

"Please, Mrs. Barlow," he said. "Sit down."

"Lieutenant, no. I came here to see Nancy. I've seen her. I'm going home."

"Okay," he said. "Do what you wish. I certainly have no authority over you to ask you to do otherwise. But I would have thought that Nancy would have been an excellent reason for your staying."

"What do you mean? You've told me she's not in danger, that she's being specially protected."

"The best protection, the only certain protection for Nancy, or any other child at that school, is to find out who killed Mary. And you might be instrumental in helping us do that."

He gestured at the chair I'd pushed back. "Mrs. Barlow, I fully understand your feelings, but please."

And slowly I obeyed.

He leaned forward, his eyes intense. "Thank you," he said. "We're in over our heads. I'm in charge of this investigation, and, quite frankly, to date, except for knowing the poor kid was murdered, I don't know anything. I haven't found evidence of any sort pointing to anyone, not even to persons unknown. All I have is that she didn't die accidentally, and she didn't kill herself. What's more, experience tells me that virtually everyone who could have done it will have an alibi, and how to find out which alibi is real and which false is going to be quite a job and will take some time. To say nothing of trying to find a motive somewhere. I'm dealing, as you must know, with a closed shop, an introverted little world of some four hundred people. And almost all of them women."

I could help, he continued, because although he was certain he eventually could discover much of what he would need to know about the school—how it ran, who was who and did what, all that sort of information—there were many other things I would know or could find out, which he as a man, as well as a police officer, might never learn. There were, for example, the sometimes inexplicable relationships girls form during their adolescence, and, conversely, their hostilities, jealousies, their envies, their pet hates and whimsical dislikes.

I couldn't argue with any of that. Nor could I argue when he said that where the staff itself was concerned, there were bound to be conflicts, tensions and personality clashes no one would ever reveal to the police. I thought of Onslow Weekes's being replaced next year as sailing "supervisory captain" by Terry Carr, and had to agree with him there, too, although I couldn't see how the conflict between them could have any bearing on Mary Hughes's death.

Ultimately, everything he said was enough to send me back to Brides Hall, but there was another reason, too, perhaps more persuasive than all the rest. Like it or not, I had been a Brides Hall student during four very formative years of my life. Because of that and because my daughter had also gone there and because my granddaughter was there now, I had to admit to myself I felt personally involved with Mary Hughes's murder. I don't think I could ever have slept easily again if I'd denied the police the kind of help I could give.

"I don't want you to do anything, Mrs. Barlow," he said after I'd told him I'd go back. "I just want you to be there so I can ask you questions as they arise, and hopefully get answers."

I told him I couldn't guarantee answers, but I'd try. And then I got that smile again. All of it, and quite unexpectedly. "Good," he said. "To start, I'll ask you one right now: Dead Monkey."

His knowledge of the horrid thing's existence surprised me. He then explained what had happened in my absence, but not everything. He saved the grotesque part for me to see for myself when I returned to the school. Now he only told me that Dead Monkey had shown up on *The Maryland Queen*. A group of younger students had found it when they had given the boat's deck its weekly scrub.

He wanted to know all about Dead Monkey, everything, and I told him. I also told him how Mary Hughes had been so terrified of her responsibility that she had hidden Dead

Monkey behind her suitcase on the top shelf of her closet and how it had disappeared on Saturday, probably taken by someone just to get her in trouble.

I told him everything I knew about Dead Monkey except the one thing I couldn't know.

I couldn't know until I saw Dead Monkey myself on returning to Brides Hall that afternoon what sort of a vicious mind had stolen it from Mary Hughes.

⟨7⟩

SOMEBODY HAD PUT a hangman's noose around the neck of Dead Monkey, had sewn a bit of purple cloth to its lips to make a protruding tongue, and had then hanged it from the rigging of *The Maryland Queen* where, head-height above the afterdeck, it swung gently to and fro with the wind. And as if that weren't a sufficient obscenity, whoever had done it had also pinned a large printed message to its rugby-shirted chest. It said:

> *Reject Mary felt so blue*
> *Without a Hubert's boy to woo*
> *And with just a monkey on her shelf*
> *She went and hanged her silly self.*

The vicious vulgarity of it left me speechless. I simply stared. Dominic asked two plainclothes detectives if forensic had done everything necessary: taken pictures, dusted nearby tackle and brightwork for prints. They said yes.

"Okay," he said. "Take it down. I want a detailed lab examination of its clothing, see what it may have picked up in the way of fiber strands, lint, dirt, stains. Also that tongue. We might be called on to match it up to some fabric if someone was stupid enough to keep whatever it was cut from." He added, "And tell lab to step on it. I want it back here tomorrow."

I don't think I had ever disliked Dead Monkey, and everything it stood for, more than at that moment. An intense anger rushed out of me. "You'd be better advised to burn the damn thing," I said.

Dominic took my arm as we walked off the deck and onto the dock. It was again a beautiful late-spring day with hardly a cloud in the sky; the air soft and filled with the indefinable perfume of fresh greenery and blossoms. A blue heron flew low overhead, feet dangling slightly, its long neck thrust forward, and a ragged flight of snow-white egrets circled over the creek. They seemed sudden, blessed sanity.

"I want it here," Dominic said. "If it's connected to Mary's murder, and it could be, I want someone to have the chance to meddle with it a second time. They might slip up and give us a lead of some sort. Who gets it next?"

"You mean who inherits it?"

"Correct."

"Probably the Head Girl," I said. "At least until she assigns it to someone new."

He flipped open a notebook he'd pulled from his pocket. "Constance Burgess, right?"

"Yes."

"I'll want her told to assign it to nobody. Where does it usually spend the summer when school closes?"

"In the library." I pointed to Main. "On the second floor."

"That's where I want it then. If the school objects, I'll confiscate it as evidence." There was a hardness in his voice. Then it softened again. "What's above the library?"

"Nothing. The Repository."

"That's not nothing, Mrs. Barlow." He laughed. "Repository for what?"

"A lot of things. Almost everything you could imagine, from old chemistry equipment to worn-out sports gear. But mostly it's used to store costumes and scenery."

"Scenery?"

"The school gives an operetta every year. Gilbert and

Sullivan usually. It's for friends of the school and for local people. The school's way of saying thank you to everyone for being good sponsors or good neighbors, and to publicize the fact that the performing arts haven't been neglected in the school's curriculum. This year's show is next week."

Dominic shook his head and I had the feeling he was suppressing laughter, that if it weren't for the fact there'd been a murder, he would have indeed laughed. He obviously found much about an all-girls boarding school comical, especially one for the wealthy privileged.

"A busy three weeks coming up," he said. "Theater, parents' day and boat races." We were now halfway back to Main. He stopped, looking at it. "I want a tour, Mrs. Barlow. Everything."

I was surprised. "Haven't you already had one?"

He smiled. "Of course. But not with the school's most attractive alumna."

That caught me somewhat by surprise, and while I wondered how to handle it, he added, "I want you, room by room, to tell me everything you know that goes on there or is significant about it."

We continued on. Silently. I was suddenly, and a little uncomfortably, aware of him as a man and not just as a police officer. When we reached the front steps of Main, he stopped again and pointed to where a heavy wall of woods flanked one side of the playing fields. "I understand that's a private bird sanctuary," he said.

"Yes. It belongs to a Mr. Randolph Balustrode."

"The trial lawyer?"

"Yes." I pictured Balustrode. I'd only ever seen him once, personally. But he was in the papers a lot, a heavyset, balding man in his seventies with an old-fashioned walrus mustache, a florid complexion and a propensity for flamboyance, bimbos and violent outbursts of temper.

"What kind of birds?" Dominic asked.

It was an idle question, unrelated to his investigation, really, but it stirred memories. "I guess just about everything going," I answered. "All the usual woodland and songbirds you get in Maryland: flickers, finches, warblers, thrushes, orioles, tanagers. And all the water birds, too. Mirgrating ducks and geese and often egrets and blue heron. Half the sanctuary is either salt marsh or swampy pond."

"You know your birds," Dominic said.

"My father was an amateur ornithologist."

"Interesting." And then, "The school must have some arrangement with Balustrode for nature studies, that sort of thing, no?"

I laughed. "On the contrary. The girls are absolutely forbidden to set foot on the place."

He looked genuinely surprised. "Oh? Why is that?"

I shrugged. "Ask Mr. Balustrode. He's twice sued when he caught the girls trespassing."

"Then some do it anyway?"

I smiled at this. "I think, Lieutenant, almost everyone does—once, anyway—while they're here at school."

Standing there at the front steps of Main, I remembered vividly, as though just yesterday, the one time I had trespassed. It had been an early Sunday morning and I went there on a mission. I had learned there was a pair of bald eagles nesting near a pond in the middle of the property, and I hoped to be able to tell my father about them when I went home. When I stole off the school grounds, I entered a dark, untouched world, a primordial woods that had rarely, if ever, seen an ax: a jungle of oaks, American chestnuts, giant tulips, beech, black gum and red maple, with here and there stands of loblolly and scrub pine. Ever cautious of deadly copperhead snakes, which I knew abounded, I made my way timorously along a narrow path used by successive classes of Brides Hall girls which wove through a dense undergrowth of fern, moccasin flower, holy bush and laurel. I remembered the heart-stopping moment when a young deer, frightened from its daytime hiding place, leapt to its feet and crashed away.

Now, I heard Dominic ask if Balustrode had a house on the property.

"No," I said. "But there's a gazebo by the middle pond. Quite a large one."

That day long ago, I had come abruptly upon the gazebo by stepping into a clearing around it. I quickly shrank back among the trees the moment I saw it, afraid someone would be there and see me—if not the ogre Balustrode himself, then, even worse, a dreaded senior. The gazebo often served as a clandestine trysting place for older girls and St. Hubert's boys during the school dances or when one of the latter found a way to cheat on a special weekend pass to Washington or Baltimore.

It was a largish, open-sided, rustic shelter, hexagonal, I think, with benches all around. It nested on a slight rocky rise so that it overlooked the entire pond. Assured nobody was there, I finally went and daringly sat in it.

I saw the eagles almost immediately. One, anyway. It was high overhead, a dark silhouette that seemed to float motionless in the morning sky. While I watched, it began a long spiraling descent, disappearing behind a grove of pine on the other side of the pond, then suddenly reappearing to swoop low and fast, wings hardly moving, just above the pond's still surface. When it reached a huge dead bald cypress, it shot up to land on a top branch, legs outstretched, talons spread to grasp the perch, its great wings sweeping backward to brake its speed.

I remember, too, seeing a pair of ospreys and, just before I left, a kingfisher atop the broken trunk of a submerged tree that projected, branchless and black, from the water like the bare mast of a sunken ship. The fish it had just caught was a silver sliver in its beak, and the icy blue of its back feathers was a sharp contrast to the black of the redwings nesting among bulrushes and swamp grass.

I stayed far too long and was almost found out because I missed obligatory Sunday service. I remember telling them, I think, that I'd fallen asleep in the library and getting away with the lie.

"We'll have to go through those woods with a comb," Dominic said. He frowned and shook his head. "We won't find anything, of course, but we have to do it."

He started to say more, but didn't get the chance. Ellen Mornay had appeared in the doorway.

{8}

"AH, THERE YOU BOTH ARE." She was smiling brightly, but in her use of the word "both" she identified me with the police, who represented the whole mess she had on her hands. In her tone was an acid undercurrent of the hostility most men would have missed—I'm sure Michael Dominic did—but not most women.

Ellen knew by now that I would be staying until after parents' weekend, reluctantly accepting my explanation that it would be best for Nancy. With a murder on her hands and having been told by Dominic that I'd been informed, there wasn't much else she could do.

I told her now that Dominic had requested a tour of the grounds and buildings. Rising to the occasion with graciousness and an air of prestigious authority, she offered us, so to speak, the keys to the campus.

Meanwhile, I marveled once more at her appearance. She looked absolutely terrific. Her clothes were expensively smart; her dark brunette hair softly shaped and . . . and that's when I finally realized that she'd had work done on her face, around her eyes, particularly, and almost certainly on her neck and jowls. Ellen had always been a conspicuously heavy-breasted woman, even as a student. She certainly wasn't any longer. She was perfectly proportioned. I hadn't really thought before to match Ellen's personal looks with her expensive clothes and sports car. Where on earth had she got that money? Perhaps an inheritance?

60

"I'm going up to Washington," she announced. "I have to dine with some of the trustees again, although they're taking it all surprisingly calmly. One of the Washington papers has got hold of your presence here, Lieutenant, but fortunately not the real reason for it, and I need to asure them everything is well in hand. The publisher is married to a girl from the class of '75, and he's promised to squelch any future stories."

She gave Dominic the sort of ingratiating smile she usually reserved for multimillionaire parents. "Margaret will be able to answer any questions you have about the school's history and functions while I'm gone," she said. "And Terri Carr knows everything about everyone currently here, staff as well as students."

I found it difficult to remain smilent. She sounded for all the world as though there were nothing more amiss at school than a minor flu epidemic. I couldn't help but wonder whether, over the years, endless school crises had developed in her a completely hardened attitude toward disaster, or whether she wasn't covering up near panic with an iron self-control.

When she'd finally driven off, I took Dominic on the extended tour he'd requested. We did Main first, starting with the dark dusty scenery and artifact-choked Repository on the top floor, followed by the large, well-endowed library which shared the floor below with Gertie Abrams's room, the school nurse's apartment and the infirmary. Next we visited all of the first floor: Assembly and study hall, the administrative offices, the faculty common room, the kitchen and dining rooms. After that we toured dormitories, schoolrooms, and the gym, where Onslow Weekes was working out on the Nautilus machine. I could see by Dominic's expression that he took as dim a view of the head coach as did I.

We finished up at the new stables after looking over the brush and wooded site beyond and to one side of the guest suite. This area was to be cleared and leveled that summer preparatory to work commencing on the Hiram Burgess complex that fall. It was late afternoon by the time we headed back for Main.

"Now, tell me about this race," he requested. "Your boat here and the boys'-school one . . . what's it called?"

"The Chesapeake," I said. "The boats are sister ships donated by wealthy alumni of both schools, and the race has been going on since 1934. It starts at the mouth of the Little Choptank at a buoy off James Island, goes south to Tangier Island a few miles down the bay from the mouth of the Potomac, and then back up."

Dominic looked both surprised and impressed. "That's a round trip of close to a hundred and twenty miles."

"They start Saturday, come back Sunday. They run all night. We have had races when they didn't get back until Monday."

"Did you ever do it?"

"Once," I said. "I was on the main jib winch."

"Did you win?"

"That year we lost."

"Do you usually?"

"Lose? No. Usually, we win."

I hated myself for the "we" and the pride in my voice.

"That must be a little tough on the boys," he said.

"That's their problem, not ours."

He laughed. And that's when he caught me completely off-guard the second time by asking me to have dinner with him.

I probably shouldn't have agreed. I am as aware as the next person of "never mix business with pleasure." I'm also aware that an "older" woman who is flattered into forgetting age difference can often be more vulnerable than she was in her younger days.

But if I'm reasonably world-wise, I'm also human and a woman, thank heaven. I'd had a bad few days, and the thought of a nice dinner somewhere with a very attractive man seemed immeasurably appealing. We arranged a time that evening, and like a silly schoolgirl, I took special pains with my hair and makeup and kicked myself for packing only practical clothes.

He took me to a lovely old inn not far from Burnham, which had first opened its doors in 1814, and still served the best broiled crab on the Bay. Candlelight reflecting off old ceiling beams and the burnished copper pots decorating the walls made everything infinitely romantic.

I'll give credit where it is due. Michael Dominic, I'm sure, had ulterior motives in asking me to dinner—his eyes gave him away—but for that evening he stuck to business. On my part, I tried very hard not to flirt, and I think I succeeded, although it was difficult not to, especially remembering the amount of vintage wine he poured. A lot of chemistry had been going on all day, and we were now on a first-name basis.

Over drinks, I told him as much about the school as I could. Then we began to talk as people do when getting to know each other. I told him about my long and happy marriage to George, which had ended nearly eleven years ago; about ballooning and gliding, and how this was partially due to George's exhortation before he died that I'd not dwell in the wonderful past we'd had together, but reach out and embrace life on my own.

"Where does that leave you with romance?" he asked.

It was a pretty leading question, and I met it head-on. "It leaves me like any other woman," I said. "Free to choose and I hope intelligent enough to know I could be in trouble unless I choose carefully."

He took that without a flicker of expression, and I quickly got off the subject of me and onto him. He told me about his architect father and his doctor mother. He'd gone to Columbia University in New York and had majored in history. "I got into this business by accident," he said. "History doesn't get you jobs and I needed one fast. I never imagined myself as a policeman, but occasionally it can be interesting. The police deal with aggression, with deviation from the acceptable social norms, and that's always fascinated me. If aggression can be turned away from ugliness, it can be extremely beneficial; it creates competition, which in turn stimulates society's creativity as well as its economy."

He was thoughtful, articulate and, in the candlelight, especially handsome, his sensitive eyes and mouth emphasized and his strong hands gently expressive.

I had a perfectly lovely evening.

It ended in heart-racing fright.

Michael drove me back to Brides Hall, escorted me to my guest-suite door and, without lingering, said good night. Before we left the car he gave me a thick manila folder containing police dossiers on most of the staff and students and on the school's employees. I couldn't believe the police had done so much in such a short time. It told me at once what sort of priority was being placed on the case. He would be very interested, he said, to hear my opinion on what I read.

I watched him walk back across the quadrangle, a shadowy, diminishing figure disappearing and reappearing under the street lamps, which broke the darkness with pools of diffused light. When his car headlights went on and he drove away, I went into my bedroom and turned on the lights, pulled down the blinds on the windows facing the pitch-black woods. It frightened me a little, I confess, all that darkness. Then, starting to undress, I got the strangest feeling something in the suite was wrong. It was as though I were not alone and yet of course I was.

I am not a coward, but it took all my courage to open the door to the clothes closet and assure myself no one was hiding in it. Then, feeling the fool, I looked under the bed and behind the frosted glass of the stall shower. Clearly I was alone. But had someone been here? The maid, yes, who had turned down the bed and again had opened my suitcase and laid out my nightgown. The maid or Gertrude Abrams. But someone else? Someone who wasn't supposed to come into the suite?

I'd planned to take a shower. My body ached with fatigue. I didn't. I couldn't. The thought of being trapped in it à la *Psycho* by a Tony Perkins proved too much for my tired nerves. I undressed, slipped into my nightie, double-locked the door, then sat on the edge of the bed and reached for my old traveling clock.

That's when I saw it. Almost instantly I felt the scream rising from deep within, to choke silently in my throat, making it almost impossible to breathe.

It was a photograph. An awful, horrifyingly obscene photograph. I always travel with a silver-framed picture of my two grandchildren, gorgeously suntanned and laughing from the deck of a sailboat. That photo had been replaced by a Polaroid shot of Mary Hughes hanging dead from the chapel balcony, her face blue and contorted from strangulation, her body a limp, shapeless rag.

Across the bottom of the photograph was written in large, bold letters: "Go Home."

{9}

I THREW THE PHOTO across the room in uncontrolled revulsion. Then, dimly realizing Michael might want to see it, I found the courage to retrieve it and put it face-down in an unused drawer in the living room sideboard. I used a handkerchief to pick it up, not for any intelligent reason such as keeping possible fingerprints from being smudged, but because I couldn't bear to touch it.

Michael had given me his personal telephone number if ever I found it necessary. Calling him wouldn't help. Whoever had done this surely was not planning to break into the Smoke House suite just then. A warning always gave someone time. My antagonist, I decided, would do nothing further that night. The best thing I could do was to keep my head, try to get some rest and call Michael in the morning.

I found my photo of Nancy and Christopher on the floor behind the bedside table, propped it up against the lamp, settled into bed and took up my book determined to read. Of course I couldn't. I turned off the light and tried to sleep. I couldn't do that either. Remembering that the guest suite was supplied with enough liquor for an army, I rose, fixed myself a stiff Scotch and water, and took it back to bed. I slowly sipped it while forcing myself to believe that every rustle of leaves in the woods behind the suite, stirred no doubt by night wind off Chesapeake Bay, was not the onset of my own murder.

I don't know when I finally fell asleep, but the Scotch

did the trick. All of a sudden, it was morning and daylight was trying to enter the room. When I opened the inhibiting curtains and let up the blinds, golden early-summer sun sifted in. How different everything always looks by day.

Just the same, I couldn't bring myself to open the drawer of the living room sideboard and take out that photo. I didn't think I ever wanted the silver frame back. No matter what picture I might put in it, I'd always only see that ghastly Polaroid.

It was still quite early. I took a shower and made myself not think about Mary Hughes. I was to meet Michael after lunch and I had a lot of reading to do before then. With blessed daylight dispelling nighttime ogres, I decided to wait until I saw him to tell him about the picture.

I dressed in the denim skirt I'd brought and the best of my blouses and a light cardigan. I was careful with makeup and my hair, and then sat a moment staring at myself in the mirror.

What on earth had come over me? I rarely ever was so concerned with myself. But I hardly had to ask the question. I knew only too well what. And why. Michael Dominic. Margaret Barlow, admitting only under threat of death to being fifty-five, was trying to look her best for a man more than ten years younger.

I came sharply to my senses, stuck my tongue out at my reflection, kicking myself mentally for being so foolish, and left for a grandmotherly breakfast with Nancy in the dining hall. After Nancy went off to class, I had a second cup of coffee with Terri Carr, who made no bones about her feelings regarding the Dead Monkey tradition, which she said was as ugly as the stuffed animal itself and ought to be ended.

"Most of the traditions of this school continue all the cloistered protection monied children usually get at home, and out in the real world that protection simply doesn't exist," she said.

I had little chance to do more than agree when the bell for first class rang and she had to go. I told her I'd come around to Assembly later that afternoon and help her with some of the preparations for the annual operetta—this year, *H.M.S. Pinafore.*

Even a brief talk with Terri gave me a lift. She was so filled with energy and optimism, and I thought of what a long road she'd come and what a different beginning hers had been from Ellen Mornay's. She'd been raised in a small coal-mining town in West Virginia, she'd told me during dinner the first night I'd stayed at the school. Her father had been a mine foreman who'd died in a mine accident when she was eight.

At the memory, her face had become terribly sad, but she'd brightened immediately. "And here I am," she'd said, "surrounded by enough wealth probably to buy the whole state of West Virginia, let alone that damned mine he used to go down every day. Do I resent it? Of course not. The girls here, for all their money, aren't that much different emotionally from the crowd I went to high school with. Money may protect, but it doesn't change human character as much as people would like to think. They may have better clothes and better meals and not have to work their guts out during vacation, but they're under the same adolescent pressures. They have all the same teenage miseries and hang-ups and frustrations."

I returned to the guest suite, where a cheerful young maid I thought about eighteen was making up the room. The school had half a dozen such domestics, and it was hard to see how most of them, unlike Terri, and in spite of sunny dispositions, didn't have hidden resentments against the far more privileged women their age they served. Surely some had to be as bitter as I felt Gertrude Abrams was.

When she was finished, I sat down in a comfortable living room chair and started in on the contents of the manila envelope Michael Dominic had given me.

Over three hours later when I put it down, I couldn't believe much of what I'd read. I knew that most people had some sort of skeleton they wished would stay in the closet—I had one or two myself. But somehow you never attach skeletons to people you know, especially if they are seemingly respectable. When you find out what they have kept hidden, and in some cases even forgotten themselves, you get a shock. Just about the only person I'd met, student or faculty, who didn't have a "past," was Gale Saunders, the unfortunate senior who had discovered Mary Hughes's death.

I read up on students first. Angela O'Connell, who Nancy told me was the school sneak and who had the crew position on *The Maryland Queen* of "ship's message runner," had been arrested by police two years before on a charge of shoplifting at Bloomingdale's in White Plains, New York. A juvenile court had remanded her to her parents with orders that a psychiatrist report on her progress at the end of eighteen months.

Where students I'd met were concerned, I wasn't all that surprised at the kind of trouble Sissy Brown had been in. She'd been expelled in her freshman year at Taft, a leading New England prep school, when caught in a boys' dorm taking a shower, to put it politely, with two young men on the varsity football team.

In spite of her broad-shouldered, six-foot frame, this somehow fitted the Cynthia I'd met. I found far more startling what the Maryland police had dug up on the school's Head Girl, Constance Burgess. I read about her twice to make certain I hadn't misread anything. Checking with police in the girl's hometown of Fort Worth, the local police had learned that her bank account there had shown two large and unexplained deposits during her sophomore year at Brides Hall, and shortly after her mother had discovered several pieces of her jewelry missing. With no evidence of any sort of burglary and no clues pointing to the household staff, the Fort Worth police had discreetly questioned Connie and got nowhere. She said she'd won the money at high-stakes backgammon, and a boyfriend, the son of a leading judge, had backed her up.

What I read about those staff members I'd met left me equally wondering about people's frailties or, in the case of Onslow Weekes, perhaps not so much wondering as disgusted. Since his marriage and the birth of his first child, now three, he'd been reported on two different occasions to be seen entering a cheap New Jersey motel with a known prostitute aged fifteen. The police had done nothing because they were waiting for the prostitute to lead them to a much bigger prey and didn't want to endanger their scam.

In a less sordid history, Arthur Purcell, the school comptroller, had once been suspected of bookkeeping irregularities at a Michigan firm, although it was never proved. I was unsympathetic with the fact that he might have been unjustly fired from his job, just as I was fairly sympathetic when I read that Terri Carr had been suspended for three months while at college for having used a roommate's credit card without her permission to buy a dress for a spring dance.

The big surprise among the staff was, of all people, Gertrude Abrams. I could hardly believe what I read. Fifteen years ago she'd been arrested for threatening to shoot a former teacher at the school. Because she was drunk—I couldn't imagine Gertie ever drinking at all, let alone drinking too much—and hysterical at the time, the school had persuaded the teacher not to press charges. I decided that out of sheer gossipy curiosity I would wheedle what that was all about out of Ellen Mornay.

Some other skeletons were amusing: a student who had impersonated a movie star to get herself and her boyfriend luxury weekend accommodations in a five-star Washington hotel; a gardener who had kidnapped a neighbor's cow in revenge for the neighbor's shooting his rooster and had the cow shut up for the night in the chapel.

It was lunchtime when I finally put the whole dossier back in its manila folder, and a very unpleasant moment I'd been dreading finally had arrived. I knew I must turn in the photograph of Mary Hughes to the police, which meant that I had to go and get it.

Taking the manila envelope with me in which to put the

photo, silver frame and all, I went directly to the sideboard and opened the drawer.

The frame was there, where I had left it, face-down. I will never know what prompted me to turn it over. Certainly I had no desire in a million years to see that photo again. It was an easy matter to slip it, back to me, into the envelope. But I didn't. Instead, I turned it over.

Nancy and Christopher, gorgeously suntanned and laughing, stared back at me from the deck of a sailboat.

{10}

IF THE HOT, sleepy farmlands of the Eastern Shore, with their vast open fields scattered here and there, with groves of pine or hardwood trees, seemed to belong to a bygone era, the waterways, a labyrinth of creeks, tidal inlets, bays, islands and rivers, are just the opposite. In spring and summer, from the head of the bay at Havre de Grace to where it meets the Atlantic at Cape Charles, the Eastern Shore teems with a bustling activity that leaves the past to memory.

At the busy commercial wharf in that prettiest of Chesapeake Bay harbors, Oxford, I sat on an empty crab pot, a large boxlike wire-mesh trap usually found underwater catching crabs. I was hardly aware of the various crabbing boats docked virtually at my feet or of any of the gaff-rigged single-masted skipjack oyster dredgers lying alongside. Nor the "Jenkins creepers," flat-bottomed "grass boats" which crabbers used in shallow, marshy places. And I really didn't see, either, the vividly contrasting counterpart to all that commercial fishing activity: the scores and scores of lovely private yachts, power and sail, being readied at marinas and in the harbor itself for another season of sailing and cruising the Bay.

Lieutenant Michael Dominic stood by me, munching on a revoltingly greasy hamburger he'd picked up at a wharfside fast-food counter. He'd given me a blow-by-blow lecture on everything great about Maryland's oystering and crabbing industries, and I was getting more and more ir-

ritated by the second. For twenty minutes I'd heard everything there was to hear about "astering," as the locals called
gathering oysters; about "seed bars" and "growth bars,"
where oysters were bred and raised, and some sort of a
killing snail called an "oyster drill" and a fungus called
MSX, which was short for some bit of biological Latin nobody in his right mind could ever hope to pronounce; and
how both snail and fugus yearly killed up to seventy percent
of the oyster crop; and how the Chesapeake Bay in Virginia
was five times more polluted than it was in Maryland, and
how that was a big problem because most of the seedbars
were in Virginia waters.

I'd had enough of the Chesapeake Bay's world-famous
crabs. Atlantic blues, two hundred million of them a year
shipped out to every corner of the globe: "sooks"—they
were the mature females—and "big Jimmies"—the
males—and hards and softs and crab floats, which is where
they kept the hards when they'd lost their shells and became
soft until they grew new shells and became hard again. And
how three trays of live softs packed in wet sea grass and
ice made up a sixty-pound box to be refrigerator-trucked
to major canning or marketing centers.

I think it was when he told me that a good crab picker—
that apparently was some poor woman whose job it was
to fish the crabmeat out of a cooked shell for shipment to
a cannery—could produce forty to fifty pounds of meat a
day that I finally blew, although I'd almost done so when
he'd launched into an ecstatic description of how some
trotlines were nearly a third of a mile long, with bait attached every three feet.

"Oh, for God's sake, Michael, will you please shut the
hell up? You shouldn't be in the police. You should be
Secretary of Commerce, or whoever it is flies the state's
fishing flag." I waved at a small open launch he'd told me
was called a tonger boat, its deck littered with broken oyster
shells and mud from the bay's bottom. "Why don't you
just drag me out to sea on one of those? Give me a practical
demonstration."

I must have sounded as ferocious as I felt because I remember he looked very taken aback and then promptly proceeded to punish me by turning to have a word with a fisherman friend, leaving me to pull myself together.

I did. He turned back.

"Sorry, Margaret. I thought it best to get your mind off things for a bit."

"I'm the one to apologize," I said. "But I really don't care right now how famous Maryland is for anything." The smile I gave him must have shown how contrite I felt because he smiled back and said teasingly, "I don't either, actually. Would you rather talk about murder instead?"

"I would not," I laughed. "But we're stuck with it, aren't we?"

"Yes, I'm afraid so."

Michael had met me at the school promptly after lunch, and sensed immediately that something was wrong. "Okay," he said. "What happened?"

When I'd told him as calmly as possible, he frowned and muttered something under his breath, I think a four-letter word, and said, "Let's get out of here, go somewhere we can talk. This place is claustrophobic."

That's how we ended up in Oxford.

He sat down beside me on the crab pot and said, "All right. Let's begin with the photo. Who took it, who had the chance to? It's probably the one my photographer reported he lost the night of the murder. The maid at your suite—she's one of ours, incidentally, and started yesterday—said whoever came in to take it away must have done so after you went to breakfast and before she got to the suite. That's a pretty risky time frame."

The maid a police officer? So much for my philosophizing about the resentful downtrodden. "Why bother?" I asked. "To scare me even more?"

"That's the most likely reason."

"They succeeded."

He looked thoughtful. Then he said gently, "I don't like this. Whoever we're looking for sees you as a danger to them, that's quite clear. I wouldn't think less of you, Margaret, if you packed up and went home this afternoon."

I said, "Sorry, Lieutenant Dominic. I appreciate your concern, but no way."

My answer, foolish as it may seem, came from my heart and not my head and was due to several reasons. One was a certain bravado, always a fault of mine; I simply never could admit there were dangers I couldn't handle. Another was because of an equally old fault, my inability to control my curiosity. And finally there was my hating to be an "outsider" when something was going on.

"Do you think that's wise, Margaret?"

I put on a laugh. "No," I said, "but then I've never been known for wisdom."

He should have vetoed me on the spot, of course. If he had, I might have got out of the whole business right then and there, before I was so deep in it pride wouldn't let me. But he didn't and I know now it was the first of several times when, in spite of himself, he would put personal feelings over professional duty. Personally, he didn't want to see me go. All I was aware of at the time was his staring at me in silence, expressionless, and finally, somewhat stiffly, I thought, saying, "Okay, suit yourself."

He busied himself turning over pages of the dossiers, then said, "Tell me your reactions."

I told him that in general, with of course a few exceptions, I thought the skeletons of those I'd met seemed out of character with how they currently presented themselves.

"Skeletons always do," he said. "Did you read anything that would give you any ideas about Mary Hughes?"

I told him no, I hadn't seen anything at all, not the faintest suggestion. "Except . . ."

"Except what?"

I tried to formulate my thoughts. "Except," I repeated, "if none of the skeletons seem to fit the people's present characters, other than Purcell's, Weekes's, and Sissy Brown's perhaps, then, looking at the school as a whole, whoever is the murderer isn't apt to seem like one. Not a brilliant deduction, but it makes me *also* think that whatever the murderer's motive, it may be one that isn't at all obvious."

"Makes sense," he nodded, thoughtful again. Then, in one of his sudden switches which I was getting used to, he asked, "What does John Ratygen mean to you?"

"He's a senior Senator from California," I said. "His wife is on the White House staff and he's also one of the school trustees."

"And went to Saint Hubert's and was captain of the varsity football team," Michael added. "Am I right?"

"Yes. Yes, you are." If I was surprised at his question, I was utterly amazed by the extent of his homework.

Especially when he said, "And dated Ellen Mornay?" It was clearly a rhetorical question.

"Good heavens," I burst out. "How did you know that?"

His eyes suddenly became hard. As did his voice. "Like it or not," he said, "I'm a police officer investigating a particularly nasty murder."

I tried to get us back to a lighter vein. "I'd hate to think you knew that much about me."

"You're not a suspect."

"Ellen is?" I failed to keep my shock to myself.

"Everyone at Brides Hall is," he replied. "From Ellen Mornay down to the kitchen staff. No exceptions. Now let's get back to John Ratygen. How serious was his romance with Ellen, and how long did it last?"

I tried to remember. It all seemed so very, very long ago. Ellen had indeed been going steady with John. But I'd forgotten until just that moment that after Christmas her senior year, she didn't go to either of the two St. Hubert's— Brides Hall dances, and everyone whispered that she'd been ditched.

"For someone else?" Michael asked.

I had to smile. "That's usually the reason a boy ditches a girl."

"It would have been a girl at Miss Porter's?"

Memory is a funny thing. The moment he said the name,

it all came back to me. Miss Porter's, in Connecticut, was at the top of the prep-school ladder and a major rival of Brides Hall. "Yes," I cried, "that was it. He started dating someone there."

"But you don't remember her name."

"I don't think I ever knew it."

"Her name was Melanie Wood," Michael told me. "Ring a bell?"

It did immediately. It conjured up a picture of a tall, handsome but aggressively hard-looking, dark-haired woman—the kind from whom most men flee. Her face was forever in the newspapers. "The White House lady," I said. "So she's *that* Melanie."

"He married her their senior year in college, and as you probably know, they're planning to divorce."

I think for a moment I simply stared because I suddenly realized exactly what he was getting at. "What you're saying is that now Ellen might be getting a second chance?" I asked.

"What do you think?" he parried.

I thought of Ellen. Everything about her bespoke a woman who'd had a tremendous emotional lift, the kind a woman usually gets from a great new romance. I thought of her smart new clothes, her new face and figure, her car and, above all, a kind of feminine self-assurance I didn't remember her ever having. "I think maybe you're right," I said.

"She's been spending a lot of money," he said. "Too much for the salary she earns. I'd like to know where it's coming from."

"Perhaps an inheritance?" I offered.

"Or Ratygen," he said. "We're checking on it. But it's not easy. You don't get too nosy around a man who carries his political clout. Not if you don't want to risk your job."

"I don't see how any of this ties in to what happened to Mary Hughes."

"You're right," he said. "It wouldn't seem to, but when you're investigating this sort of a case without a single clue to go on, when everyone seems to have a perfect alibi for the time the crime was committed, and when you can't find a trace of motive anywhere, your only recourse is to build as much of a picture as you can of everyone, no matter how unimportant that picture may seem, and hope something turns up. In my experience, something usually does."

We headed back shortly after that, neither of us saying much on the way. But when we reached Brides Hall and parked in front of Main, Michael broke a long silence. "I want you to promise me one thing, Margaret," he said. "If anything like this happens again, you won't wait five minutes to tell me. You'll get in touch right away."

"Fair enough," I said.

He looked relieved. I opened the door to get out, paused, then said, "And, Michael . . ."

"What?"

"Thank you for telling me everything I ever wanted to know about crabbing and 'astering' but was afraid to ask."

He laughed, and I went into Main to meet Terri.

{11}

IN ASSEMBLY, school workmen had already put up the temporary stage that annually spread across one end of the big former ballroom. It was no small affair, nor was the production the girls put on. The school had a first-rate drama and dance coach, and among three hundred and fifty students almost anywhere, there's always a fair amount of amateur talent. One soon became so immersed in the combined genius of Messrs. Gilbert and Sullivan that it was easy to forget the cast of the Brides Hall production was composed entirely of the female sex.

Half a dozen seniors were rehearsing a scene, including Constance Burgess and Sissy Brown, who were almost always together, something I found a little odd. Were they really good friends or somehow an unholy alliance? Under the existing circumstances, I was beginning to find myself always ready to suspect the worst. I was glad they were busy because I also found it a little embarrassing to face both of them, knowing what I now did about them.

I didn't see Terri Carr, but I wasn't long in finding out that she was upstairs in the Repository. Angela O'Connell appeared from nowhere to inform me. She was a sophomore, fifteen years old, a short girl, pudgy rather than seriously overweight, with a pasty complexion and a lot of braces on her teeth, which looked as though they could have used a good brushing. Her eyes were small and mean and narrowed when she spoke. She sidled up to me with an expression at once sycophantic and know-it-all. "If you're looking for Terri, Mrs. Barlow, she's in the Repository taking inventory of all the props we'll need.''

I said thank you and opted for a freight elevator to get there, since I was certain Angela would tag along if I took the stairs. She had that sort of look on her face. The elevator, located in a cloakroom by the stage, was a creaky antique which enabled scenery and props to be stored up in the Repository during performances, since behind the stage it was too cramped. The Repository, which doubled as a dressing room, took up half the attic space of Main. It was a hot, stuffy place directly under a huge sloping roof. Everything pertaining to the theater when the operetta was actually in production was kept relatively close to the elevator, which was not far from the stairs. The props were on six long rows of floor-to-ceiling steel shelving which were divided by a center aisle. The scenery, over forty big and little canvas flats, slid into deep racks built for that purpose.

It was a badly lit place, full of dark corners where one could hardly see, not because of insufficient lighting fixtures but because of the amount of things stored there. The number of shelves and the great number of things on them inhibited the overhead lights and prohibited practical lighting of any other sort. Some help came from four dormer windows at the rear of Main, one of which led to a fire escape and was always left partially open for safety reasons. It proved over the years to be a front door into the building for mice, squirrels and the occasional bird. Some of the same unwanted wildlife often went farther than the Repository, finding their way downstairs into the library, which lay directly below and was reached by a little iron spiral staircase usually shut off with a hinged trapdoor, often left open by forgetful students.

I found Terri in jeans and an old sweatshirt beyond the last row of shelves, going through one of a dozen racks of old costumes and pulling out dust-covered sailor suits to mark down the different sizes against a list of girls in the cast. I wasn't exactly dressed for doing much more than holding the clipboard while she called out sizes and, later, furniture.

While we worked, she told me all about the production, who was playing what and whether or not they had any talent and who could never remember their lines. Eventually the subject of the new auditorium came up, and I learned of friction between Terri and Ellen Mornay over Constance Burgess. It was a little like pulling teeth to get the full story; Terri was a discreet person and didn't want to appear disloyal. I didn't want to seem too nosy about school matters that were really no concern of mine. I went at it slowly, and soon Terri told me that the cause of the friction was Hiram Burgess's fondest wish that Constant attend an Ivy League college and Ellen's consequent pressuring of Terri to make this possible.

"But it's not possible," Terri said. "Connie's grades simply aren't up to it, and nobody from any prep school has carte-blanche entry into the Ivy League these days, or to any other top college, for that matter. Not the way they used to. Ellen just can't seem to understand that. Besides, it's too late anyway. College applications went in last year and students were either accepted or rejected by last fall. Ellen insisted on Connie applying only to the Ivy League, regardless of my insisting she was shooting too high and should go for less academically competitive colleges. Of course, the result was that Connie got rejected everywhere, so it's Texas State for her. It can't say no. She's a state resident with adequate grades for acceptance there. How Ellen thinks I can reverse that, I don't know. She keeps having me write letters to various deans to try to set up new interviews or find out if they'll take Connie in exchange for an endowment. But it's too late. What's done is done."

"What's Ellen trying to get out of Burgess?" I asked. It seemed the logical question. Why else would she be making such a fuss? "I mean, I would have thought the new complex was enough."

"But that's just it," Terri replied. "The deal on the complex is seventy-five, twenty-five. The seventy-five percent is to be put up by Burgess and we're to match it with twenty-five percent from the school's endowment. But Burgess said he'd pay a hundred percent if Connie made it to Princeton or Harvard, and Ellen would like to leave the endowment untouched. That would be quite a coup for her where the trustees are concerned."

That indeed was a revelation, and I tried a chance shot in the dark. "Especially with John Ratygen?" I asked.

Terri stared a moment, surprised, and then her answer came: a quick smile before she turned away to hide it. "You said that, not me." And she busied herself with the furniture again.

I decided not to pursue the matter and cast out a closing remark on the Connie Burgess problem. It had, I said, a classic ring to it. To my surprise I came up with more information, not about Connie Burgess but about Sissy Brown. I don't really know why Terri told me what she did. I think partially to cover her confusion over discovering I suspected Ellen and John Ratygen.

She reappeared from behind furniture and laughingly said, "You're right, and that makes two classics around here. We have another that in a way is the exact opposite— Sissy Brown. Straight As and A-pluses. Besides being a great athlete she's an absolutely brilliant student. She's going to graduate cum laude for sure, and she was accepted by both Princeton and Harvard. You couldn't hit a bigger jackpot. And we'd give anything to expel her."

"Oh?" I was hardly surprised and immediately pretended a gossipy interest. I couldn't, of course, say that I knew she'd been kicked out of another school and why.

"She's a terrible influence on a lot of girls," Terri said. "She hates us, hates being here, is constantly belittling the school and its rules to the underclassmen. We're almost certain she's been carrying on with Onslow Weekes. Curtiss told me he thinks he nearly caught them at it in the gym one evening last week."

That Weekes could have been so foolishly, or compulsively, indiscreet did surprise me.

"Weekes? But he's married."

Terri smiled wryly. "Yes, he is. And his wife is a lovely person. But he's after any young girl impressed enough to give in to him. He's one of those. Sometimes I can hardly bear to look at his wife, poor thing. She must know."

"But I wouldn't have thought that of Sissy," I protested. "She hardly seems the type, does she?" Then I remembered the way he had looked at Connie Burgess and Gale Saunders the first night at dinner. "Besides, I thought he was interested in Connie or Gale Saunders."

Terri laughed again. "I know," she said. "You caught his looks at dinner. I saw you." She shook her head. "He probably is but can't get either of them, especially Gale, and he doesn't have that problem with Sissy." She sighed. "She's been in trouble for that sort of thing since she was quite young. She was sent off to boarding school when she was fourteen because of trouble with the family chauffeur and promptly got into more trouble there with some boys."

I asked why the school didn't get rid of Weekes.

"For the moment," she answered, "the same reason as trying to get Connie into a college that will never accept her. Money. Weekes had *The Maryland Queen* winning races, at least he makes everyone think so. Four years in a row now. To some of the alumnae that means a lot. Last year we got a fifty-thousand-dollar prize from one of them for our victory."

I wondered briefly how much the alumna would have given if she'd known Weekes visited sordid Jersey motels with fifteen-year-old prostitutes.

"But that's coming to an end, isn't it?" I asked. "I understand this is his last year."

Terri nodded. "Yes. Ellen and I have decided that the danger of Weekes's feelings about young girls far outweighs any joy he might bring the alumnae. If one of his little flings got known or if he got some girl pregnant, the school would be in dire trouble. So removing him from the *Queen* is the first step in possibly removing him altogether."

Suddenly, she looked desperately anxious, and I realized at once that the possibility of my repeating the confidences was bothering her.

"It's all right, Terri," I said. "Anything said to me stops with me. I can promise you that."

She studied me a moment, then impulsively leaned forward and kissed my cheek. "Thank you, Mrs. Barlow."

I felt the worst sort of cheat because I knew that eventually I might well pass on everything I'd learned from her to Michael Dominic, and Terri was the one person around who deserved to be leveled with, a lonely voice of realism, I thought.

To my relief, we didn't get a chance to speak further. A group of girls came up on the elevator, laughing and chattering and saying they were ready to work.

Feeling frustrated, I went off to keep a date with Nancy for tea at the Burnham Inn. In spite of Michael Dominic's apparent confidence that ultimately, if enough pictures were drawn, something important would surface, I couldn't see anything. I felt up against a solid wall of perhaps interesting but totally unimportant information. Absolutely nothing I had heard or observed seemed in any way to relate to poor Mary Hughes.

I was wrong. Everything I had seen and heard related directly to her death, and to my chagrin it was that horrid little Angela O'Connell who pointed me in the right direction.

{12}

SHE WAYLAID ME a second time, poisonous creature that she was, right after I dropped Nancy off at Main a few minutes before study hall.

"Mrs. Barlow?"

I stopped with an instant sense of being trapped.

"Mrs. Barlow?" she repeated in a suitably conspiratorial tone. "You're a detective, aren't you?"

My reply was polite but firm. I managed a pleasant smile and said, "Good heavens, no!" I tried to move on; we were in the doorway of Main, and she blocked my way.

"Yes, you are," she declared. "Nancy said so."

"Oh, I see. Perhaps that's because Nancy thinks I should be." I made a mental note to chastise my granddaughter, then edged past her.

Unfortunately, she danced along beside me down the steps of the columned porch and onto the gravel driveway as I headed for the guest suite. "I could tell you something about Mary Hughes that you'd be interested in, Mrs. Barlow."

"I'm sure you could, Angela," I said perfunctorily. I kept walking. She kept tagging along.

"I know something about Mary I bet I knew before anybody else."

This time I didn't answer, but she next said, "I know where she was all afternoon so Sissy Brown could get into her room and steal Dead Monkey."

That stopped me. "Sissy Brown?"

85

"Oh, sure. Sissy either stole Dead Monkey herself or had her freshman do it for her."

We were standing by the chapel now, to me already slightly sinister-looking in the late-afternoon light, with the awful memories it held. "Angela, that's a rather serious accusation to make. If you're sure about it, though, don't you think you should speak to Miss Mornay or Miss Carr?"

Her answer was to smile spitefully. "Mary didn't hang by accident, I bet. I bet someone hung her. Twisted the rope around her neck and . . ." She rolled her eyes and put out her tongue and made a strangling sound.

Speechless, I just stood staring at her hateful, pudgy face.

I finally managed a few words. "Now, Angela, I'm sure you don't really mean that. Why would anyone want to do such a thing?"

"Because she must have seen something."

Alarm bells rang in my head. "Seen something? Where? When?"

"Or maybe took a picture."

"Angela, please come to the point."

"When she went to Balustrode."

"Nobody's allowed on Balustrode," I reminded her.

She smiled again, and I thought, how horrible that a child this age could already be so sly. "The seniors all go there with Saint Hubert's boys," and added meaningfully, "to the gazebo."

"Did you see Mary go to Balustrode?"

"It was Saturday afternoon. She had her binoculars and a camera. She went bird-watching. And she had a tape recorder, too."

I suddenly had an odd pit-of-the-stomach flutter. "Are you sure about this, Angela?" I asked.

Her answer was a slow, triumphant grin which lit up her mean eyes. "See? I told you you'd be interested."

I could tell she had nothing further to say, and I needed to be alone to mull over what I had just heard. I glanced at my watch and pretended alarm. "Angela, thank you for the confidence, but just look at the time. You'll be late for study hall. We'll talk more later.''

I gave her my warmest look of appreciation and walked away briskly, forcing myself not to look back because I knew she'd be standing right where I left her, waiting to see me do just that. It was hard not to shudder at the thought of what sort of woman she'd grow up to be.

I had dinner in the dining hall that evening at Ellen Mornay's table. She had again stayed in town, thank heaven, but still I found it acutely uncomfortable to be seated at a table with people whose secrets I now knew. I could hardly bring myself to face Onslow Weekes, let alone talk to him. And Arthur Purcell appeared shadier than ever to me. Neither Connie Burgess nor Sissy were there. They'd returned to their regular tables and I was grateful for their absence, especially Sissy's. Halfway through the meal, I suddenly and for the first time thought: *You could be sitting here with a murderer*.

I had coffee in the faculty room with Terri, and we were talking about the new complex when it dawned on me that Mary, during the awful Inquisition, might have had to give an accounting for her actions that day. If so, and if Angela was right that she had gone to Balustrode and might have heard or seen something someone didn't want seen or heard, could she have told the assembled seniors what it was?

Terri was called away to a college-application conference with a junior, but before she left I asked her if Angela O'Connell was given to making up stories.

"No, I don't think so," Terri said. "She's a lot of things, that one, as you must have gathered, but I don't think she lies. In fact, quite the contrary. She takes a sort of wicked joy in always being dead certain that the tales she tells are the gospel truth. Run afoul of her, have you?''

"She cornered me today with a story about Mary trespassing on Balustrode just a few days before she died. The day Dead Monkey disappeared from her room.''

Terri shook her head. "She regaled me with the same story the day after the Inquisition. I'm afraid I was rather short with her. I told her that Mary had suffered enough at the hands of the seniors and that neither Ellen, who concurred when I told her later, nor I would be interested in seeing her punished further."

I finished my coffee and headed back for the old Smoke House. Halfway across the quadrangle, I stopped short. It was twilight, the first stars were out and the sky was mauve with oncoming night. There were lights on now in the old slave quarters turned dormitories. I looked up and saw Constance Burgess talking to someone by her window; I couldn't make out the other girl. I decided to see what she could tell me. As Head Girl, she would have attended the Inquisition.

Gale Saunders opened the door to my knock; she was Constance's roommate. Constance, now at her desk, rose at once, and when I apologized for disturbing her and wondered if she could spare me a couple of minutes, was instantly hospitable. So much so that it was difficult for me to believe her capable of stealing her mother's jewelry. And why would she have needed to? Didn't she already have everything any girl could ever want? Her stereo looked like the most expensive model money could buy, and I'd heard her father had given her a brand-new Maserati convertible for her sixteenth birthday.

When I told her what I wanted and that I'd also like to see Sissy Brown, she betrayed discomfort for only the most fleeting instant; then, all heartfelt good manners, asked Gale to get Sissy.

Cynthia Brown came in immediately—it turned out her room was next door—and without Gale, who had not been present at the Inquisition. One look at me and Sissy was instantly on her guard, which I felt was a clear giveaway of guilt. I was at once hopeful and got directly to the point. I knew they'd both seen me talking at length to Michael Dominic and that they both must have wondered if my coming to see them had anything to do with the police investigation. I didn't plan to give any reasons unless they asked. If they did, I'd decided to say that a group of parents had delegated me to investigate unofficially, but there would be no report of the interview made to the school.

They didn't ask me. At first I thought it was because I was an "old girl" and they were confident of my automatically respecting the secrecy attached to the Inquisition tradition. It soon became clear that I was wrong. I found myself confronted with another tradition: the seniors' unspoken code of silence, "the wall." I got nowhere.

"You didn't ask her where she'd spent the afternoon?"

"I don't think so, Mrs. Barlow. Why would we have?" Constance answered.

"Did anyone suspect she might have gone trespassing on Balustrode, for example?"

"Oh, I doubt she would have done that, Mrs. Barlow. I mean, we all know lots of girls used to in your day, but nobody does anymore."

Delivering that line, Sissy Brown wore a positive smirk, and I was willing to bet almost anything that she'd spent plenty of time at the gazebo with Onslow Weekes.

It went on like that for half an hour; question after question fell before the wall. Once I nearly lost patience. "You both sound as though there'd been no Inquisition at all," I remarked.

A sweet smile from Constance Burgess, the Texas accent more pronounced than ever. "Mary was a very lonely and sensitive girl, Mrs. Barlow. We took it real easy on her."

"The Inquisition isn't nearly as tough as it used to be," Sissy said.

It took everything I had not to get nasty, so I accepted defeat. I thanked them for their time and left them staring after me when I went out the door, Constance with a wide-eyed look of innocence, Sissy Brown with her smirk.

But out on the quadrangle, after I'd taken a few deep breaths, I realized that in a way the smirk belonged to me. Both girls had been so busy "walling" me and feeling triumphant at their success that I don't think it ever occurred to either that their wall was in itself interesting. Unless they had been walling me just for the sake of doing it, and I didn't think that was so, then they were hiding something.

Meanwhile, of one thing I was dead certain: Mary Hughes had indeed trespassed on Balustrode and her trespassing could well be connected with her death.

The next morning I showered and dressed quickly. I had something I wanted to do that day which I'd decided on just before I fell asleep the night before.

I would go to Norfolk, Virginia, three hours south. I intended to pay a call on Mary Hughes's mother.

⸭{13}⸭

THE DRIVE FROM CAMBRIDGE down the Eastern Shore to Norfolk, Virginia, is interesting, and some of it spectacular.

From Burnham and the Little Choptank River in Dorchester County, I took a long, straight state highway to Salisbury in the middle of the Delmarva Peninsula, then swung south. After a while, as the peninsula narrowed and became Virginia, the low flat countryside gave way to windswept seacoast. And when I arrived on the peninsula's long narrow trail, ending at Cape Charles and with the Atlantic Ocean only a mile or two from the highway, I was suddenly in a world of the sea itself. There were sand dunes and scrub pines and dune grass, and it seemed to me both ground and air were filled with gulls, shore birds, waders and waterfowl.

The Chesapeake Bay Bridge, going from Cape Charles to the Norfolk area, is eighteen miles long, an extraordinary combination of trestle highway and tunnels, into which the road dives deep under the Bay's Atlantic mouth from manmade islands, allowing easy access to the Bay for large ocean shipping.

Coming off the bridge, I made my way through the heavy urban traffic of Virginia Beach, then Norfolk, getting lost twice before I swung north again across another bridge over the great naval harbor of Hampton Roads, which seemed to be occupied by half the United States Navy. Paralleling the James River, I drove through Hampton toward the famous colonial village of Williamsburg.

91

The Hughes family lived in Jefferson Park, a modest suburban development just as Hampton gave way to countryside. I found it and found Wright's Lane and then number 43, a small brick ranch house set back from the street by a well-kept lawn and some lovely flower beds.

I parked, went up a flagstone walk to the front door and rang the bell. When nobody came, I rang a second time and finally heard approaching footsteps. There was a rattle of locks and a chain being taken off, and the door was opened by an exceptionally attractive, slender, dark-skinned black woman about my age. She was wearing a housedress and an apron, and the smell of cooking came down the short hall behind her. I apologized for disturbing her and asked if Mrs. Hughes was home.

"I'm Mrs. Hughes."

"Mary Hughes's mother?" I was so surprised I could barely speak.

"Yes."

The question brought her close to tears, and I noticed her eyes were already red from weeping.

And then the years suddenly fell away as I recognized her and she recognized me. I couldn't believe either my eyes or my memory.

"Sally."

"Yes. Oh, Margaret, Margaret!"

We threw our arms around each other and she started to cry, and I guess I did, too.

We went inside like that, arms around each other, I babbling my reasons for coming, she telling me how glad she was to see me and how well I looked, both of us talking at once and holding each other's hands. Then we sat down on a couch in her living room and for a moment just stared at each other.

"I can't believe this," she said finally.

I said I couldn't either. "When did you marry?"

"Oh, about five years after you graduated." She told me about meeting Jake Hughes, a young machinist-mate sailor who was making the Navy a career and taking courses to get a specialist rating in rocket maintenance, and was now a chief petty officer. She'd been Sally Shepherd then, a pretty sixteen-year-old maid working at her first job at Brides Hall. We became friendly when I discovered she loved reading, and I would take books out of the school library for her, dozens of them eventually.

That friendship became something more one spring night in my senior year during an annual Brides Hall–St. Hubert's dance. Some of the boys had got hold of liquor and become rowdy. One, thinking he was terribly funny—"Just to see if they float," he said—deliberately poured a glass of dark fruit punch down the cleavage of my white dress, the only one I had, putting an end to the dance for me. Soaked and furious, I left Main to cross the quadrangle to my room, when I heard muffled sobbing from among the shadows of the chapel, and boys' laughter. I ran over and found Sally cornered by three St. Hubert's boys. They'd drunk too much and were out of control; one had already ripped open her blouse.

Without thinking that there were three of them and only one of me, I sailed into them, and I don't remember exactly what happened because everything blurred into scrambling, scratching, lashing blows, and the harsh scream of my own voice. They fled, of course. In the darkness I didn't get a good enough look at their faces to be certain of identifying them, and later Sally begged me to say nothing. "When you're black," she told me, "you learn real quick that this kind of thing gets turned around and you get accused of asking for it."

I took her back to my room and gave her one of my blouses to replace her torn one. Two months later I graduated and our lives went separate ways, the way people's do; a few long letters, then just Christmas cards and finally not even that.

Until I knocked on the door of 43 Wright's Lane today.

I'd expressed my condolences and she'd made us both some tea. I could no longer hide my confusion. I'd never heard of a black family adopting a white child, and said so.

Most agencies would have made it impossible for them to do so even if they had wanted to.

She smiled with genuine amusement. "How a black woman ended up with a white daughter? Easy. Ellen Mornay arranged it. Just like she arranged for Mary to go to Brides Hall."

"But why Ellen? Mary wasn't hers, was she?"

Sally smiled. "No. But close."

"Whose, then?"

Her answer left me speechless. "Gertrude Abrams's."

"No."

"Yes."

"Who was the father?" And even before the question was half out of my mouth, I knew the answer. It had to be the teacher Gertrude had threatened to shoot.

"Apparently he got his kicks from succeeding with the impossible ones, and Gertie was harder than most," Sally explained. "I guess if she ever wanted a man it had to be her most secret fantasy and probably only a one-second fantasy at that. He gave her the full treatment—she was the only woman he ever truly loved; he was going to leave his wife and children for her, all that. We've all heard it once in our lives. Most of us anyway."

"And when she found herself pregnant and he didn't leave his wife," I said, "she threatened to shoot him."

Sally nodded. "Oh, she carried on all right. I think it was the only time anyone ever felt sorry for her. Ellen had to shut it up or risk a real scandal. She'd finally turned the school around, and newspaper publicity about one of her staff was the last thing she wanted. By the time Gertrude got around to making a scene, because at first she'd just kept hoping and pretending it wasn't true, it was too late for an abortion. Then, when Gertrude finally had the baby, she was scared that if she gave the child out for adoption to a regular agency, she'd never be able to see it again. So Ellen asked me if I'd take Mary, unofficial-like, and I couldn't have children, so I did."

I listened and felt pity for Gertrude, and at the same time

the deepest respect for Sally for taking on what must have been a burden in raising a child of a different color.

"Did Gertie interfere much?" I asked.

"You know, I was afraid she would," Sally answered, "but she almost never did. It's as though once Mary came to me she didn't want her anymore. Yet when it was time for high school, she decided Mary was going to go to Brides Hall, come hell or high water."

"To spite the place? To get her own back?"

"I think probably so. She went to Mornay and threatened her, said this time she'd sell the story to the newspapers, and of course Mornay gave in at once. It was no big deal for Brides Hall to take on another scholarship student. Jake and I were happy to have her there, even though they gave her a hard time because it meant she was getting the education we couldn't afford to give her. And then this. We loved her so. Oh, Margaret, you would have, too. She was so good. So very, very good."

I said nothing while she broke down. I thought of Mary and the warm, loving home she must have had; you could feel it in every corner of the room we were in. I thought of Sally and her husband's decency; I thought of love and heartbreak, the years of parental protection and care all ending one evening in an impersonal call from a policeman. The disbelief at first, the shock, then the dark storm of total grief.

And I thought of the child's other mother, that strange, twisted woman, and the sorrow she must be hiding. There had to have been some spark of love in her for Mary, something a little more than just getting her own back for all her years of envious semi-servitude in a monument to the spoiled, privileged children of elitist parents. Hadn't Nancy said Gertrude was Mary's only other friend, and that she often went to the housekeeper's room for cookies and cocoa? How far removed from the reality of all that were Constance Burgess and Cynthia Brown, I thought.

The police had told Sally that Mary had been murdered. Michael Dominic had driven down and had had the decency to break the news gently to them himself after the funeral.

"He's a nice man," Sally said. "He'll find whoever it was. But I don't understand, Margaret. Why would anyone want to kill Mary? Why?"

Why indeed!

I had learned from the school office that all of Mary's personal effects had been packed up and sent home. On an odd hunch, I asked Sally about her camera.

"They sent it down. With all her other things." She looked at me, suddenly curious. "Why do you ask? Someone at school called up yesterday—I don't know who, they didn't say—and wanted to know the same thing. And when I said yes, they wanted to know if there was still film in it—something about maybe there were pictures of the school they could use; they said Mary was a very good photographer. But there weren't any. She'd always brought her film here, you see, at the local shop. The man used to give it to her at cost if she let him display the shots she took as advertising because she was so good. She finished up her last roll and sent it down to me to be developed."

"Did you?" I asked.

"Oh, yes. There was nothing. Just pictures of flowers and birds, mostly in the woods."

Woods! I felt a tremor of excitement. That could be Balustrode if Mary had indeed taken her camera with her there, as Angela O'Connell said.

"Was it a man or a woman who called, Sally?"

"It was a woman."

"Could I see them?"

"Of course." She went to a sideboard and came back with a Kodak envelope of three-by-fives.

I began to look at them, one by one. The local photo shop was right; so was Brides Hall. Mary took lovely pictures with a rare sense of subject and composition, and with considerable technical skill. Her flowers seemed living, breathing things that leapt out at you in swirling patterns of color, and her birds, caught with a telephoto lens, were exquisite. I felt a renewed anger at the callousness of the girls who had bullied and rejected someone of such sensitivity and talent.

The sixth and seventh photos I looked at made me hold my breath.

Both were close-ups of a wood thrush, it's russet back and heavily spotted white breast unmistakable. It was perched on the blossoming branch of a wild cherry tree, and in the background by each photograph, surrounded by trees but slightly out of focus, was a small, open-sided rustic building I at once recognized as the Balustrode gazebo. Two blurry figures were just visible standing in it, their backs to the camera. The head of one was obscured. The other, hardly more than a shadow, had on what appeared to be a blue jacket. Indeed, it took me a moment even to realize it was a person. Had Mary been aware of whoever it was as she took the pictures? Perhaps not at first, in her concentration on the wood thrush. But I suspected then she had, and, terrified of being caught, had sneaked away.

I told Sally that the two photographs might be of importance and asked if I could take them and the negatives to the police. She agreed. I then asked to see Mary's tape recorder. If Mary had recorded the wood thrush's song, she might also have picked up background voices which in turn might reveal the owner of the jacket and perhaps even something said that wasn't supposed to be overheard.

Sally shook her head. "She didn't have a recorder. We were planning to give her one at Christmas."

Could Angela have been mistaken? She seemed to have been right so far. "Did she ever tape bird songs?" I asked.

"Oh, yes, all the time. But she usually borrowed a recorder for that." And then understanding what I was after, she said, "There weren't any tapes with her things. I have a couple here, but they're from last fall. Migrating geese as they flew overhead. And some other bird songs. Margaret, who do you think that is in the photos?"

"I don't know, Sally."

But I intended to find out if it was the last thing I did. I rang the school to check on Nancy and to give her a message I'd be there to take her out to a late dinner. They were having dress rehearsal for the operetta that evening, and Nancy wasn't in the performance or needed backstage. I had lunch with Sally and spent the afternoon with her. I know a little of grief. Death of a truly loved one is something you never completely get over. Some of the awful void always stays with you, but you learn to live with it, accept it, and get on with life until it's your own turn.

I think I helped Sally. I made her talk about Mary and what she felt, persuading her not to button up inside her the terrible blow she'd suffered. When I left, I took her gift of one of her favorite photos of Mary and herself, both their faces filled with laughter and joy, and that made up, in part at least, for that other dreadful photo.

⦃14⦄

ON ARRIVING BACK AT SCHOOL, I called Michael but was informed he had gone to Washington. I didn't want to discuss what I'd discovered with anyone except him, so I left a message for him to call me. Next I very carefully hid Mary's two photos, along with their negatives, in a place I doubted any intruder would even think to look: under two pictures in an album of school photos I had found in a bookcase.

In the morning after breakfast, there was the usual frenetic activity and sense of urgency around Main that always preceded a performance of the annual operetta. Dress rehearsal the night before had, as it did every year, shown up weaknesses in certain performances which needed to be strengthened: cuts that had to be made; difficult scenery changes which had to be rehearsed again or reworked entirely; costumes that needed refitting or repairing; makeup which needed a new approach because it hadn't shown up well in the stage lighting; and adjustments to be made in the lighting itself.

It was Wednesday; there were no classes, and those who weren't in the show or involved in its production were to be found in their rooms; on a pass allowing them to wander about Burnham or Cambridge until six in the evening; or out on the playing fields.

Or, in the case of Sissy Brown, on board *The Maryland Queen*. Sometime during the night I became determined not to be walled by Sissy and Connie Burgess any longer.

I was certain both had plenty to tell me, and I had decided
Sissy was the most vulnerable. Bullies are often cowards,
and when confronted with a few harsh realities, usually
cave in. If Connie had indeed managed to thwart the Fort
Worth police, she would be, in all likelihood, a much
tougher target. I was told Sissy was preparing charts for the
big race with St. Hubert's on parents' weekend, and thus
I once again found myself heading across the playing fields
for the boat houses and the wharf.

When boarding the schooner with Nancy, I'd been too
anxious and worried about the child to think much about
the boat whose very existence was of such major importance to every single girl at Brides Hall. More than anything
else, it represented the school's spirit to such an extent that
to every girl the *Queen was* Brides Hall.

The Chesapeake Bay packet boat—until the Civil War
there were several dozen—was especially designed to de-
liver mail, passengers and light cargo in days when land
routes were usually not much more than rutted wagon
tracks, and progress from one city to another often was far
faster and less hazardous by sail.

Because of the shallow water in many of Chesapeake
Bay's harbors and inlets, the boats, sixty feet on the water-
line with ten-foot bowsprits for carrying flying and outer
jibs, were built with a centerboard rather than a keel, their
hulls relatively flat-bottomed and drawing only four feet.
The centerboard, a massive adjustable keel like a huge flat
plank, is raised and lowered through a slot in the boat's
bilge. Housed in a solid casing which dominates the boat's
center below decks, it divides the main saloon, along with
the massive trunk of the main mast, into port and starboard.
It is dropped when making into the wind or quartering to
prevent slippage and raised going before the wind and
when ghosting into anchorage at port.

The shallow draft of the boats means that for the most
part, "below decks" are at least half "above deck," head-
room in the main saloon being made possible by a long

cabin housing rising two and a half feet above the main deck of the boat, with portholes forward and on both sides and entered aft, a short distance from the helm, by a door-hatch and a ladder.

In creating two replicas of the famous boats, one for Brides Hall and the other for St. Hubert's, the yacht builders had been faithful to the original in almost every detail except for the installation of two modern "heads," a small Gray diesel motor, and a modern galley with a four-burner butane stove and a relatively large refrigerator. Oil lamps had been replaced by electricity, and the settees in the saloon were, I suspect, far more comfortable than the originals had been.

I found Sissy below, seated at the chart board in the portside navigation section of the main saloon. Onslow Weekes was there, too, but if anything had been going on between them, which I had the impression had been the case, they'd managed to separate by the time I set foot on the bottom rung of the ladder. Weekes, wearing Sissy's crewman's blue beret he'd forgotten to take off, was on the other side of the centerboard bulkhead from her, fussing over an electronics manual which I figured he had hastily got from the "control cabin," a small space by the engine room. Strictly off-limits to both captain and crew, it contained up-to-date electronic navigational gear, radar and radio telephone, all monitored as a safety precaution by Weekes. It was only to be referred to in case of disastrous dead-reckoning navigational errors by the girls or a serious emergency, such as an on-board fire, requiring outside assistance.

Obviously I couldn't talk to Sissy with Weekes around, even though I knew he'd probably hear everything I had to say later from her. There was nothing to do but ask him to leave. So, after a few courteous opening remarks I certainly didn't feel like making, I told him I'd like a private conversation with her and asked him if he'd mind leaving us alone.

He didn't care for that, not one bit, but he muttered something about having plenty to keep him occupied in the gym. His eyes, as he departed, wished me to disappear magically off the face of the earth. When his footsteps had sounded on the deck above and on the gangway leading onto the wharf, and when I'd seen him through one of the portholes of the cabin coaming strutting onto the playing fields to intercept a couple of lacrosse players, I turned to Sissy.

She obviously suspected what was coming. Deliberately squaring her wide shoulders, she crossed her muscular arms over her chest and stared at me with an expression of scorn tinged with outright dislike. I thought how terribly frightening she must have been to Mary Hughes; no doubt she must be to most of the students.

I sat down across the chart table from her. "I'm not happy with the answers you gave to my questions of the day before yesterday," I said, coming right to the point. "I think the time has come when you had better decide to be more frank and stop walling me."

She stared me right in the eye and said, "Nobody was walling you, Mrs. Barlow."

I decided to take a shot in the dark that I was almost certain was a safe bet. When Angela O'Connell heard Mary Hughes was to undergo an Inquisition, she could not possibly have kept her knowledge of Mary's going onto Balustrode armed with a camera and a tape recorder to herself. The wretched little child would have been eager to tell someone in authority. That meant a faculty member or one of the seniors, Connie most likely, as Head Girl, with Sissy Brown a safe bet for second choice, since Angela knew very well, as did the whole school, how Sissy felt about Mary.

"Let's start at the beginning," I said. "Mary's trespassing on Balustrode."

"But I told you, Mrs. Barlow, I don't know anything about that."

"That's not what Angela O'Connell says. Angela says she told you all about it."

I hit home. The smirk suddenly vanished. In the moment's silence before she answered, it was replaced by ugly sullenness. "She must have told someone else. She never told me a thing."

I put on a smile I didn't feel. The more I saw of this girl, the less I liked her. "Sissy, do you really think after our meeting the other night that I'd bother to question you further if I wasn't certain of getting answers?" She started to speak. I held up my hand warningly and went right on. "Why do you suppose I picked you to talk to and not Connie? Because I think you're more honest? Don't make me laugh. You're a liar and a rotten bully, and I've got enough on you to have you on a plane home tonight if I choose. Okay?"

"Like what?" The tone was surly and still defiant.

"Like your having sex in the gym one night with Onslow Weekes."

I watched the color slowly drain from her face until she was the pastiness of dirty chalk. She tried a last bluff. "Who told you that?"

"Curtiss saw you."

Some of her color came back. She had fight in her, I had to acknowledge that. "I don't believe you."

"You'd better."

"Why didn't he report me then?"

"Curtiss is part of the school," I said. "It's his whole life. A win by this boat is as important to him as it is to everybody else. And Curtiss knows changing captains just before the race could lose it. But I'm not Curtiss. Outside of having a granddaughter here, I don't give a damn about Brides Hall. I haven't been to a class meeting in years. I'm prepared to go straight to Ellen Mornay and swear I caught you and Weekes just now on board this boat. Weekes will be fired and you'll be expelled. So make up your mind right now."

It was the only hand I had to play, and I thought it a relatively feeble one. A more worldly-wise girl would laugh in my face. But she wasn't worldly-wise, despite her posturing. She got very red in the face, the muscular arms unfolded; the wide masculine shoulders slumped and she looked dumbly down at some spot on the chart she'd laid out before her.

After a moment, she said, "Why don't you ask Miss Mornay? I already told her everything Mary said she did on Balustrode. Over a week ago."

Ellen briefed on the Inquisition by Sissy? That caught me completely by surprise. "When was that?" I demanded.

"I just told you. The day after the Inquisition."

"And why did you go to see her?"

"I didn't. She called me into her office."

If Sissy's first revelation had startled me, this one caught me even more off-guard. Inquisitions were sacred, privileged senior ground, and strict school tradition stipulated that no faculty member could ever question any senior about what went on in them. I'd stumbled onto more than I'd expected, but I acted as dumb as possible. "Oh? Why?"

"She had me on the mat for Dead Monkey."

"Then how did Balustrode get into it?"

Sissy shrugged, as though my question were ridiculous. "I don't know. I guess Angela O'Connell had told Terri about Mary going there and Terri told Mornay."

"And Miss Mornay asked you?"

"I guess."

"How?"

"What do you mean, *how?* I can't remember *how.*"

"Try," I said acidly.

I waited.

"I don't know," she said finally. "She was away in New York, and she said she didn't like that sort of thing going on when she wasn't here. I just remember telling her Angela was right. Mary confessed she went to take pictures of birds and got frightened off by two people in the gazebo having an argument."

"And?"

"And then I got a long boring lecture on how Balustrode was forbidden to all the girls, and how it was my duty as a senior—if I had any sense of responsibility at all, which she doubted—to tell her who Mary said they were."

"And?"

"And *what?* How could I tell her which girls? Mary didn't know. She only said she cut out fast the moment she saw them and before they spotted her."

"And that's what you told Miss Mornay?"

"I just told you I did."

Sissy had reached a point where further questioning about Balustrode could become counterproductive. She could even start suspecting my real reasons for asking them, and I didn't want that. Besides, I had no need to question her further. I'd gotten far more than I'd ever hoped for. Dead Monkey obviously was only an excuse Mornay had used for summoning Sissy to her office. I realized I'd almost forgotten about the dreadful creature.

"All right," I said. "Last question. What did she have to say about Dead Monkey?" I waited.

Sissy finally spoke. "She told me to return it."

"How did she know you had it?"

"She didn't. She just said if it wasn't returned and she ever found out I was the one who'd stolen it, I'd be expelled."

"So you returned it."

No answer, and I headed for the ladder to the deck above.

She stopped me, eyes frantic. "You won't tell Miss Mornay I told you? I mean, about asking me what Mary confessed? She said if I ever spoke to anyone about it, she'd put me on suspension again."

Probably not, I thought. *Probably that was Ellen just threatening.* Suspension of Sissy meant she wouldn't be able to graduate, besides not being able to captain *The Maryland Queen.* And not graduating meant Mornay would, in all likelihood, have her at the school another year.

I said, "I'm not Angela O'Connell," and went up the ladder to clean air and sunlight, trying to make sense of what I'd learned.

I was baffled by Ellen's pursuit of Mary's trespassing when Terri had told me they'd decided not to because the child had been punished enough by the Inquisition, and then her unprecedented step in breaking school tradition and questioning Sissy. Surely it must mean more than Ellen's simply wanting to find out whom Mary might have seen on Balustrode. Of all people, Ellen knew that half the girls at Brides Hall trespassed. The school did the best it could to stop it, but couldn't constantly monitor everyone and so had to turn a blind eye most of the time and hope the girls wouldn't be caught by Balustrode's caretaker or, worse, Balustrode himself. Why the acute interest all of a sudden? Was it because she was also trying to catch faculty members? Perhaps Onslow Weekes, whom she also wanted to get rid of?

I had no answers. Just questions.

At lunch, I asked Nancy who in school might have lent Mary a tape recorder. "That's a hard one, Margaret," was the reply. "Nearly everyone in school has one, but not many would lend theirs, especially not to Mary."

She made a list of names of girls she thought could help, however. There were only nine in all, but it took me the whole afternoon to find everyone, and I got nowhere.

I'd given up when I spotted Terri coming out of Assembly, heading for her office. I joined her, and when I told her what my problem was, she was thoughtful a moment and then said, "Have you tried Gertrude?"

Of course, I thought. *Gertrude.*

"Does she have one?" I asked.

"I think so," Terri said. "I think she uses one for laundry inventory, that sort of thing. Saves a lot of writing for her."

I went to Gertrude's room. She wasn't there. The whole

school was to have dinner early, and I guessed she'd gone to the kitchen to help with preparations. I knew she was due up in the Repository to assist girls with costume changes during the production. I would talk to her as soon as the final curtain fell.

⟨15⟩

AFTER DINNER I returned to my room to get ready for the evening ahead. The telephone's red message light was lit. I checked with the school operator, who told me Lieutenant Dominic had returned my call of last night. He'd said he'd be out for the evening but would I try to call him before I went to bed. I wrote a note to myself not to forget, rested awhile, then dressed and made it back to Main and the Assembly theater with five minutes to spare before opening curtain.

Taking my seat, I surveyed the audience and those still filing in through the double doors from Main's spacious front hall. There were well over two hundred guests, a pleasant-looking crowd, most dressed in their daytime best for the annual event. The school had always maintained good "town and gown" relations. Any deviation from best behavior by the girls in Burnham or Cambridge was cause for immediate discipline. A chronic offender was usually expelled.

I saw faces I recognized, in spite of the years that had gone by. These were once totally familiar people: a local baker, a garage owner, the caretaker of the Balustrode sanctuary, the owner of the Burnham Inn. They looked as they always had—just older. And less authoritative than they had appeared to me when I was a student.

As the last of them were finding their seats, the overhead lights dimmed and the small student orchestra—a piano, cello, clarinet and two violins—began to play the overture.

Moments later, the curtains parted and I settled in to watch the seventy-ninth Gilbert and Sullivan performance given by the school.

In spite of the Brides Hall production being without the benefit of a single man, thus presenting the rather unnatural spectacle of immature young females playing the parts of doughty males, the performances were good. After the final curtain fell, all of us in the audience loudly showed our appreciation.

When the Assembly lights went back on, the room was filled with smiles and laughter. I imagined that backstage there were the endless exuberant compliments being showered on the show's lead performers.

It wasn't discovered until most of the audience had left that even before the final curtain fell, there'd been a second murder.

I was standing near Assembly's wide double doors chatting with Terri Carr, who had been backstage separating some props lent to the school before they got mixed in with things to go on the freight elevator up to the Repository. I saw Ellen Mornay appear in the hall, I thought from the direction of the stairs. At almost the same time, I heard one of the girls calling for her.

I don't think the panic in the girl's voice got through to me immediately. Or to Terri. But the girl herself appeared from the cloakroom, sheet-white and shaking uncontrollably from head to foot. I don't think I've ever seen anybody shake like that.

Terri rushed to steady her. "What's wrong? What's happened?"

The girl tried to answer but was nearly incoherent. Something about blood and the freight elevator. Then there were screams and we turned to see two girls, ridiculously out of place in stage makeup and sailor costumes, stumbling and running among the rows of empty chairs, completely hysterical.

Ellen approached, and Terri said, "I think there's been an accident of some sort."

Before Ellen could speak, Sissy Brown appeared from the cloakroom and called us. Her knees and hands were stained with blood. "Miss Mornay? Could you come here, please?" She was icily controlled but her voice was unusually high-pitched.

Ellen, Terri and I all went to her at once.

When we got to the cloakroom, we found another girl there, one of the younger stagehands. She was standing with her back pressed against a wall, eyes riveted to a slowly growing, already large pool of blood coming from under the elevator door. The girl was catatonic. I heard Ellen say, "Get her out of here and to the infirmary at once." She was speaking to Sissy Brown and Gale Saunders, who'd suddenly appeared from nowhere. "Quickly. And get everyone else out of Assembly."

Terri repeatedly pressed the elevator call button. "I don't think it's working," she said. "Unless Gertie's got the doors open."

Most of the floor was covered with blood by now, and when I looked at Ellen, she was as white as one of the students. "Oh, my God," she said. She turned without a word and left the cloakroom. Terri and I followed. There was no need to talk. We knew where Ellen was going: up to the Repository.

I don't think any of us wanted to be the one to open the door there, but Ellen did; Terri and I went in after her.

The light in the Repository, as I've explained before, was not very good, especially if one's eyes were accustomed to a brighter room. But for the performance, temporary lights had been strung near the elevator, where there was now a jumble of scenery and props, some of which I'd seen on stage downstairs only a little while ago. Just beyond was the elevator. Its door was opened but the elevator wasn't there. All three of us started toward it, Ellen leading, when she stopped dead and a hoarse animal sound came from her, as though she'd been struck in the stomach.

Lying on the floor in the pool of white light thrown down by the temporary lighting was a bundle of bloodied rags and a head, like a large doll's or a puppet's, with gray hair.

We went slowly to it, all three of us, and I felt that awful, deep-down, terrified anticipation I always feel when I am certain I'm going to be witness to something really bad.

I was right. What was there was Gertrude Abrams. Or half of her. Her upper half. She'd been caught somehow by the descending elevator and sheared in two just above the hips, the elevator dragging out her intestines and eviscerating her but unable to pull all of her down, as she was anchored by one hand wedged between the legs of a tier of heavy steel shelving.

The lower half of her was in the elevator itself, which had jammed near the library floor below, its roof showing through the open doors of the shaft.

Gertrude's mouth was open, her eyes bulging, her skin a bloodless gray. All her blood had run out of her and down the elevator shaft, to seep under the door into the cloakroom.

I heard someone being sick. It was Ellen. I felt faint and then Terri's arm was around me, steadying. We turned away.

My head cleared. "I'm okay," I said.

Terri said, "Ellen?"

"Sorry," she said. "I'll be all right now. Let's go down."

Constance Burgess, two teachers, and Arthur Purcell and Onslow Weekes were in the front hall. Terri said she would call the police and left immediately for the faculty common room.

"What's happened?" Weekes said.

"There's been a horrible accident," Ellen said. She had regained complete control of herself now and was calm. "It's Gertrude."

Weekes and Purcell exchanged looks and then they both went up the stairs. The two teachers, both women, started to follow. Ellen stopped them. "No," she said. "Stay here." She turned to Connie Burgess. "The faculty will be meeting immediately. You're in charge of the school until told otherwise. I want everyone in their rooms. Notify your dorm

monitors right away. Anybody who disobeys is on immediate suspension. They're all to stay in their rooms until I
give the order for them to come out."

"Yes, Miss Mornay."

"Off you go."

"Yes, ma'am."

Constance went off quickly, pausing as she left the building to say a word to Curtiss, who appeared in the front
doorway. After Sissy Brown had turned the girl in shock
over to the school nurse, she had found him in a temporary
parking area set up on the playing fields where he'd been
supervising the departure of guests' cars.

Mornay told him what had happened. "Terri's calling
the police. Lock the cloakroom and don't let anyone leave
this building."

"Yes, ma'am. Do you think it was just an accident?"

Mornay looked at him sharply. "I don't want to hear
that question again, Curtiss. From anyone. And I want no
talk among your people or grounds employees. Pay particular attention to the press. They're not to set foot on the
school grounds, and if I hear of anyone speaking to them
without my authorization, that person will be looking for
another job immediately."

"Yes, Miss Mornay."

I must grudgingly confess I was impressed by the way
Ellen took charge. From being literally sick at the horror
of what we'd seen just a few mintues before, she had
quickly got herself under control. What a mess she had on
her hands, I thought. With Mary revealed as murdered,
nobody was going to think Gertrude's death an accident. I
certainly didn't. One murder could somehow be handled,
but two was an entirely different matter. Two would not
only be certain to cause a major disturbance in the orderly
routine of the school, but even place the whole future of
the school at risk. As Headmistress it would all fall on her
shoulders. She'd have a deeply disturbed board of trustees
to cope with, some of whom might well identify her with
disaster, no matter how unfairly. And Lord only knew what

sort of field day the press would have. They couldn't be stonewalled forever.

Finally and certainly not least, there were the parents. Among both present and future ones, Brides Hall could be deemed an unsafe place to send a child. Unquestionably, Ellen would face the withdrawal of certain girls almost immediately.

Most importantly, however, she considered her responsibility to the student body to be her number-one priority. She had a major decision to make. Send the students home, or carry on as usual? I didn't envy her, especially with parents' weekend looming. Keeping the girls in school would be considered by many to be taking an appalling risk with their security. Sending them home would be an admission that the school was not a safe place.

She left for her office after telling Curtiss to round up all the staff and send them to her office at once. The police soon arrived, Michael Dominic in the first car. I was never so glad to see anyone in my life.

{16}

ELLEN DECIDED that seniors and juniors were to stay, sophomores and freshmen were to be sent home, with the sole exception of Angela O'Connell. Because she was *The Maryland Queen*'s message runner, her parents gave permission for her to remain for the race. My granddaughter, of course, was included in those leaving. Curtiss's security force was to be doubled. It was also decided to hold parents' weekend, coming up in a little over two weeks, for the two upper forms.

After I'd made all of Nancy's arrangements and spoken to her mother, I sat on the wide front steps of Main waiting for Michael. He had quickly muttered a few words about seeing me later, after the initial fingerprinting and other routine police work.

At around 2 A.M., he finally showed up, looking drawn and exhausted. He sat down on the steps next to me.

He was silent for a few moments and then he said softly, "I hate this goddamned job. I've had it with the evil-mind department. I'm going to pack it all in after this." And then abruptly, almost harshly, "Any idea who did it?"

Of course I didn't have. He asked me where I'd been when it happened, and then I told him everything I had seen or heard. He listened intently, chin resting in his hands, elbows on his knees. Once or twice he straightened to make a note on a folded sheet of paper which he had pulled from his pocket.

"Figuring the flow of blood," he said when I'd finished,

"she would have died about the time of the final curtain, perhaps even after, when the cast were taking their bows. How many calls?"

"Four."

He made some quick mental calculations. "Enough time for someone agile and quick and very clearheaded to whip up to the Repository, slug Gertrude unconscious, open the elevator doors, put her in position, then dash down the stairs, call the elevator and appear back on stage or join the crowd leaving Assembly."

"Was she unconscious then? I mean . . ." I couldn't bring myself to say more. Words made pictures in my head, and imagining the descent of the elevator on Gertrude's prostrate body, the sickening jar as it connected and started its awful work, was more than I could bear.

"Before the elevator?" Michael said. "Oh, yes. Whoever did this hit her first—with a ten-pound lead window sash. Then dragged her to the elevator and jammed her hand between the shelving legs so her whole body wouldn't be pulled into the shaft and possibly stop the elevator from moving. Can you imagine all that? Doing that to someone? Why not just hit her again and let it go at that? The first blow already fractured her skull. I'll tell you why. This was meant to look like an accident. That's one reason. The rational one. The other reason is that we're dealing with a mind that is totally insane."

"I don't understand about the elevator," I said. "How can it run with the doors open?"

"Oh, most of them can," he said. "Engineers need open doors sometimes to work on them. The security system can be bypassed, usually with a key. In the one here there's just a switch."

"But how do you know whoever did it wasn't upstairs all the time?"

"I don't know," he answered. "But I doubt it. We know we're dealing with someone here at school, not an outsider, and his absence might have been remembered later if he were up there very long. In fact, it almost certainly would have been. But," he added, "I'll guarantee you that every single person in this school has an iron-clad alibi for the time of the murder, just as they did with Mary."

I found it difficult to speak, but knew I had to. I had so much to tell him. He helped me get started by reminding me I'd called him.

I then told him about Angela, being walled by Connie and Sissy, my visit to Sally and somebody from school calling to see if there'd been film in Mary's camera; about the pictures I'd brought back with me, and learning from Sissy how Ellen had tried to find out if Mary had seen others also trespassing on Balustrode and who they might have been.

He listened carefully and then said, "That's quite a piece of work, Margaret. Did you bring the negatives?"

"Yes."

"I'll see what our lab boys can do with them. A really big, fine-grain blow-up might shed light on who was out there in the gazebo. Meanwhile we'll have to look to see who owns a blue jacket. There ought to be a few around, no?"

"There should be dozens," I said.

He smiled wryly. "Naturally. Like alibis. Everyone will have one. Now—the tape recorder. We've already been through Abrams's room with a comb. There was a recorder, all right, and we found a tape in her bookcase, too, but it was only Abrams dictating linen-closet inventory."

Dead end. Unless, he explained, the forensic experts discovered an assailant's skin or hair under Gertrude's fingernails. This was doubtful, since she'd been hit from behind and there'd been no struggle. Traces of dirt on the Repository floor that matched the dirt in the treads of sneakers worn by someone in the cast or acting as a stagehand would also be difficult to find, given the number of people who had been in the Repository that day. And to find traces of a fabric of some sort on Gertrude's clothes that didn't match up with hers would be virtually impossible, since between students, staff and employees, there were well over four hundred people at Brides Hall.

Summing it all up, Michael didn't seem at all confident that they would find anything.

"You know," he said, "there are so many murders every year which are never solved. I get the impression sometimes that any intelligent, cool-headed person can kill and get away with it if they plan carefully and cover their traces well."

"So what now?" I asked.

He laughed. "I ask you out to dinner again," he said.

There was such a non-police intimacy in his tone that for an instant I almost forgot murder and horror. I was seated on the steps of a beautiful old plantation house late on a soft moonlit night with a man whose charm and masculinity were like irresistible magnets. Part of me wanted to reach out to him, and part of me said, *Don't, you're both moving far too quickly and one of you has to play anchor.*

"That would be nice." It sounded trite, but I couldn't think of anything else to say. I stood up, and he did, too. "But I'm terribly tired," I added.

He took my arm and we walked silently to the old Smoke House. I gave him the pictures and negatives and he checked out the guest suite before leaving. "You'll be all right tonight," he said. He smiled faintly. "Too many cops around."

We were standing in the open door, very close. Too close. His eyes were locked on mine. I felt I was rapidly losing control of the situation and suddenly didn't care.

But he must have. He abruptly broke contact and stepped back outside. "There's somebody else, isn't there?"

I thought of New York and the rather special man in my life at the time. Both seemed very far away. "Let's talk about it another day," I said.

He nodded. "Will I see you again?"

I laughed, partially from release of tension, partially because of his anxious expression.

"Of course," I said. "I'm going gliding this Saturday but coming right back afterward. I'll call you."

That surprised him. I realized he must have thought I was driving Nancy home to New York the next day and would remain there. It hadn't occurred to him that I would do otherwise. I didn't give him a chance to say what I was almost certain he would, namely, that I shouldn't come back at all because Gertrude's murder meant a greater danger at school than either of us had reckoned on, perhaps especially to me.

I said, "Good night, Michael. And thanks for asking me to dinner again."

I stepped back quickly then, before it was too late and I might not be able to, and closed the door.

Going to bed I felt a bit of a fool, and then I reminded myself that I'd probably done worse things in my life than have my head momentarily turned by Michael Dominic.

{17}

THE FOLLOWING DAY, the school emptied of half its students, I saw Nancy off to New York with the teacher taking a group of girls there and then, along with everyone else, tried to settle back into a daily routine, which, for me, certainly wasn't difficult, as I had nothing to do except keep my eyes and ears open. On both Thursday and Friday, I spent time in the library and did a lot of thinking that got me nowhere. The police were keeping a low profile, and I saw Michael only twice, and then only at a distance with some of his staff.

Saturday morning I rose early. I had a three-hour drive before me. I was due at the glider field in Virginia at noon for the return engagement with my Vietnamese friend.

I got my flight gear together and hurried up to Main. It was nearly eight o'clock, the sun up for over an hour. There were classes Saturday morning at Brides Hall. The first was at eight-thirty, but here and there some girls, finished with breakfast, were already heading for classrooms.

I'd reached my old station wagon and had just put my carryall in the back when I heard my name being called. It was one of the secretaries, running toward me with a bundle of letters. "Oh, Mrs. Barlow, would you mind dropping these off at the post office in Burnham when you drive through it? They're from the faculty mailbox. I forgot to give them to the mail truck last night, and the truck won't make another pickup here again until Monday."

I said that of course I wouldn't mind and she handed me

the letters, perhaps twenty in all, held together with a rubber band. I put the packet on the front seat next to me, and, to my shame, promptly forgot all about it.

My mind was on other things. All the way to Front Royal I tried for the hundredth time to make sense of everything I'd learned since arriving at the school that might have bearing on the two murders, and perhaps even produce some clue as to a possible motive for them.

The more I thought, the more difficult it was for me not to presume, just as Angela did, that Mary had died because of something she had seen or heard at the gazebo or because someone thought she might have photographed the two people there.

What other possible reason could there be to murder the poor child? She might not have been liked or accepted, but she was totally innocent, insofar as I knew, of ever doing anything to anyone that could arouse them to murder. Even Sissy Brown must have enjoyed more than adequate revenge during the Inquisition for the trouble she imagined Mary had gotten her into.

Who were those two people at the gazebo? And what were they doing there? Would the police photo lab be able to come up with some sort of positive identification? I wasn't very hopeful. Blow-ups sometimes made things less clear, no matter how fine-grain. It depended on the original photo. No lab could improve on something that wasn't there in the first place. Had one of those shadowy, blurred figures been the person who had tried to discover from Sally if Mary had taken pictures and then murdered Gertrude, too, for fear, or even knowledge, that Mary might have confided in her?

And why on earth was Ellen so interested? That question continued to baffle me more than ever. Did Ellen know something or suspect something that had been going on at the gazebo that she wasn't telling to anyone? And if so, why wasn't she? Did she possibly know something that might put her life at risk, too, and had decided her only safety lay in silence?

The questions remained frustratingly unanswered, although I managed to put them out of my mind during a glorious afternoon's flying, where I was once again bested by my friend but this time by only several hundred feet.

It was when I climbed behind the steering wheel of my station wagon for the return journey that I discovered the packet of letters still lying on the front seat. My friend had come down by train from Philadelphia, and I'd promised to drop her off at the station in Washington on my return trip to Brides Hall. I decided no serious damage had been done; most of the letters would probably reach their destination sooner if mailed there than in Burnham.

We reached the capital about seven in the evening, and after I'd left my friend I stopped by a mailbox, took the rubber band off the package and began to shoot the letters through the slot one or two at a time.

As we all know, sometimes the littlest thing will unexpectedly cause major revelations about something else on which it has no bearing whatsoever. In this case, it was a postage stamp. Or, to be more accurate, the lack of one. I caught one letter a staff member had failed to stamp, and because she had, I stopped to check carefully all the rest in turn. As a result, I ran into something I never would have found otherwise; nor, I'm certain, would anyone else have.

A self-addressed business-reply card of a Washington furrier caught my eye. I knew the name well. It was the Cartier of the luxury fur trade, with stores in New York, Houston, Paris and London. I couldn't imagine anyone at Brides Hall, except Ellen, who could be its client, and I turned the card over with understandable curiosity. It was a request from the furrier for a time and place to pick up a mink coat for summer storage. The name the client had typed on the card was "P. Jensen," with, oddly, a Georgetown address in Washington: 11A Twenty-ninth Street.

I mentally shrugged off the card, continued checking letters for stamps and, just before I reached the end, came to one that stopped me dead. The envelope was formal school stationery, the addressee a Patricia Jensen, Architectural Consultant, and the address exactly the same as the furrier's client: 11A Twenty-ninth Street, Washington, D.C.

Although I couldn't understand exactly what I'd stumbled onto, I had a hunch it was something interesting, perhaps even important. With Michael desperate for any kind of lead, I threw all scruples to the wind, went back to my wagon and unsealed the envelope, easy enough to do by simply rolling the slender pencil of my address book under the back flap, leaving it undamaged as it came loose so I could reseal and mail it if it proved harmless.

But it wasn't harmless. It was a formal letter from Arthur Purcell acknowledging services rendered by Patricia Jensen as consultant on the new Hiram Burgess complex, along with a Baltimore Bank check for twenty-five thousand dollars drawn on the Hiram Burgess Fund and signed by Ellen Mornay.

I dropped both card and letter into my handbag, mailed the other letters, and headed straight for Georgetown.

Traffic was heavy, and it was nearly dark when I swung off Pennsylvania Avenue onto M Street and then branched off again up into Georgetown on Thirtieth. I had friends working at Georgetown University and I knew the area reasonably well. I thought 11A would probably be near the top of Twenty-ninth, where it ended in a T-junction with R Street, running along Montrose Park and the Oak Hill Cemetery, one of the highest points in Washington.

Like Twenty-ninth, Thirtieth Street is lined with trees which by day shade its beautiful old houses and at this hour helped screen out fading daylight. I parked halfway between Q and R streets, and walked up to R and around to Twenty-ninth.

Being blond has its drawbacks. Blond is far more visible than brunette. I felt terribly exposed and wished fervently that I had a scarf to cover my head. I quickly found 11A, an old Victorian private residence. The top two floors were in darkness, but lights were on in what clearly was a living room on the ground floor which had two windows facing the street. The curtains had not been drawn, and I could see most of the furnishings and pictures were in expensive good taste.

I took a chance and, heart pounding, I went up the front steps. Three different bells told me the building had been turned into apartments. One, indeed, was for a P. Jensen, and it was on the ground floor. I hurried across the street, looked about for someplace to watch. I was lucky. The house almost directly across the way was for sale and shut up. It had a small front garden; among the weeds and dead flower stalks of last year was an inactive stone fountain.

I went and sat down on it. My view wasn't perfect, a couple of dead branches partially obscured the front door, but it was better than no view at all or being completely exposed myself.

I began to wait, wondering if I had not been totally impetuous. I was desperately tired and the night was beginning to be quite cool. I was soon tempted to go back to Brides Hall, hand the card and letter over to Michael Dominic, and leave the rest to him.

Something made me stick it out, though; stubbornness, perhaps. I was already there, and I had the strongest of hunches to prove valid, so why not give it a chance? I waited for what seemed an interminable time. In fact, it wasn't all that long, perhaps only an hour, when I saw a familiar car being parked almost right in front of me on my side of the street.

How Ellen Mornay didn't see me sitting in the little front garden, I don't know. When she finally got out of her Alfa Romeo, she couldn't have been more than fifteen feet from me. She walked across to 11A and, producing keys from her handbag, let herself in. The front door closed behind her. Moments later, she reappeared at the window of the living room and drew the curtains.

Two hours later I was back at Brides Hall, by now far too tired to do much thinking. The only thing I felt certain of was that I finally knew where Ellen was getting her money. My own feelings were a mixture of excitement and shock. Excitement over my discovery, shock that Ellen Mornay seemed involved in filtering school money into her own pocket. How this tied into the murders of Mary Hughes and Gertrude Abrams, I had no idea.

The school grounds were dark when I drove through the main gates, with only a few lights on in Main and the dormitories and the usual old street lamps around the quadrangle and going down the path to the Smoke House. I hadn't expected this and I immediately felt uncomfortable. Brides Hall was usually well lit until midnight. Telling myself the place was dark because half the students weren't there only made things worse.

I parked my car and began to walk to my room. There was a slight night breeze coming off the Bay up the Little Choptank River and Burnham Creek, bringing with it a smell of salt water and rustling the leaves of the elm trees around the quadrangle. I cut across the lawn to avoid the chapel, stopping once when I thought I heard one of the chapel doors creak open. Nobody came out; the doors, barely visible in the near dark, seemed shut, and I went on.

I was by now quite nervous, even frightened, and I became more so when I found the street lamp outside the Smoke House not working. The absence of light made the Smoke House seem excessively dark and foreboding, and, looking back, the other quadrangle lights now appeared very, very far away, too much so for comfort. I felt completely isolated and alone. By the time I'd got out my keys and reached the door, all the paranoia I'd shed in the air over the Blue Ridge Mountains and in Washington had returned with an icy and paralyzing grasp. I almost couldn't breathe and nearly fled back to Main.

I didn't. I unlocked the door and pushed it open into the guest suite's pitch-dark living room, fumbling for the wall switch next to the door frame, expecting I don't know what—I think a hand to grab mine.

The lights went on. The living room was untouched— or appeared to be so. I looked into both bedrooms, the kitchenette and bath. Everything seemed normal. The bed in my room was turned down, my nightgown laid out as usual.

And then I finally noticed. There was something wrong with the smooth surface of the bed near the footboard, a certain rise in the covers. A hot-water bottle put there by the maid? It was far too large for that. And the weather too warm.

I went to it and reached out to feel the covers, but my arm froze halfway. I couldn't bring myself to touch whatever it might be. I stood by the bed, indecisive, a nameless dread of the unknown rising in me. I couldn't *not* know what was there. I couldn't get into bed unless I *did* know. I couldn't go up to Main and find a security guard and bring him back to discover there was nothing more dangerous in my bed than a folded blanket inadvertently made into the bed by the maid who'd readied the room for the night, the most likely explanation, since the maid had probably been Dominic's detective.

Suddenly, I got my courage up and, with a kind of frantic defiance, seized the covers and yanked them back.

What lay under them was a heavy folded black rubberized something. I think even before I flipped it open I knew what it was. But it took doing that before my realization sank in all the way, and the horror of it rose up my throat and pounded in my inner ears.

What someone had put in my bed was a bloodstained body bag.

⦗18⦘

I DON'T KNOW HOW LONG I stood there by the bed in the sort of transfixed state I've always imagined a rabbit to be in when confronted by a snake.

The bag held me like that, motionless, as though in its awful blackness it were alive and compelling me to obey. As every second passed, it became more and more an expression of everything I'd experienced over the past week; a mirror image of the photograph of poor, broken, rag-doll Mary Hughes; of the ghastly imitative shadow of Dead Monkey swinging slowly back and forth over the scrubbed white deck of *The Maryland Queen*, and above it, the ugly creature itself with that vicious message pinned to its chest; of Gertrude Abrams's head and shoulders and mangled torso, a bloody bundle of crushed and legless rags on the Repository floor, her lifeless skin gray-white and that dreadful red stream of what had been her life flowing slowly down the walls of the elevator shaft and out onto the Assembly cloakroom floor.

What I felt most of all was revulsion. It crept in and over me, slowly at first, a gripping kind of nausea that had a feeling of its own, a dark cold oiliness. I was nearly sick and I felt incapable of moving. But I did move, finally. I reached for the telephone, and my personal phone book in which I'd written down the emergency number Michael Dominic had given me. I could think of nothing else but doing that. Everything in me concentrated on it.

126

I found the number, I lifted the receiver.

The line was dead.

My revulsion instantly became fear; the room around me sharp with it, clear, everything in it standing out as though it had individual importance. Did I expect the front door to burst open at any second? I think so. I had to get out of there quickly before that happened. I was alone. Help was hundreds of yards away. I grabbed my phone book and purse and rather foolishly, I suppose, seized a heavy vase of flowers by its neck and, mindless of the water that poured out of it and the flowers scattering on the floor, marched through the living room of the suite to the front door and yanked it open.

Ridiculous Margaret. Nothing more dangerous greeted me than the dark wall of the night, broken here and there as in an Impressionist painting by small patches of light from street lamps or distant building windows, daubs of yellow-white on a black canvas.

I didn't run. I walked. Frightened, yes. Oh, most certainly. But acutely calm at the same time. I knew that running would give me away; that if someone was watching me I couldn't give them the satisfaction of knowing how I felt. Of course, I never thought that by still gripping the vase and by not closing the suite door behind me, my emotional state was fully revealed. At such times, one tends to have an odd perception of reality.

I made it across the darkened school grounds when there was the sudden beam of a flashlight on the colonnaded porch of Main. It danced in irregular patterns like a living thing, alien and threatening, then went out when a rectangle of light from within the building shot out over the porch as someone opened the front door.

Even at a distance, I recognized with relief that the hand which did this belonged to Curtiss. There was a second man with him, the paunchy state trooper who had become a familiar fixture in my daily life. The two of them were an island of unexpected sanity.

Curtiss heard my footsteps on the gravel drive and, just as he was about to close the door, peered down the shaft of light, recognizing me. "Hello there, Mrs. Barlow; thought you'd be abed by now."

"My telephone's not working," I said. "And I have to make a call." I went up the steps onto the porch.

The trooper had taken his hat off and I saw that he was quite bald, with only a fringe of hair above his ears and back of his neck. It made him look far less law-and-order and his ever-present, low-slung six-shooter ineffectual.

"There's one in the faculty room," Curtiss offered. "That's the nearest, anyway. I think Miss Carr is there. Working late."

I thanked him and went down the short corridor to the faculty room, with its heavy leather chairs and couches and chintz curtains. Neither man seemed to have noticed the vase I still gripped tightly by the neck, and I put it down on a table.

Terri was indeed there, asleep in a chair, a pile of paperwork fallen from her lap to the floor and an empty cup of coffee on the table beside her. I hated to disturb her but had to, and she awoke with a start the moment I softly spoke her name.

"Margaret. Hi. I thought you were still off gliding."

I remembered that I'd told her I might spend the night in Washington.

"I decided to save the hotel bill," I said. "Terri, my telephone is out of order. Is it all right if I use this one?"

"Of course." She got up, rubbing her face. "I guess I fell asleep. Would you like some coffee? I'm living on it." She picked up her cup.

I told her I would. Making coffee would get her out of the room for a few minutes. I really didn't want an audience when I talked to Michael, although Terri was the only person I would have trusted to hear what I had to say.

She disappeared and I sat down with the telephone and dialed the number he'd given me. It rang and rang and rang. Then his voice came over the line, heavy with sleep.

I was merciless. "You said to call anytime. I need to talk to you."

"Go ahead."

I told him about the body bag. It didn't take long, but something occurred while I was talking that completely broke the unique and protected tunnel world between two people that a telephone makes possible. One moment I was telling Michael that when I'd gone to call him I'd found the telephone dead, the next I heard him cup his mouth-piece and say something to someone. That's when I realized he wasn't alone. A woman.

I was suddenly out in the cold again, unprotected, a kind of very intimate trust I had in him gone.

"Margaret? Hello?"

I said I was still there and mechanically repeated every-thing I'd already told him when he asked me to go over it again.

Then he said, "Okay, now listen. I want you to act as though nothing has happened. And don't tell anyone. Un-derstand? Nobody. Can you find another place to sleep tonight?"

I thought of Nancy's room and told him I probably could.

"Okay. Just don't go back to the suite," he said. "I don't want anything touched there. The reason you give is the telephone. And me. I said you couldn't because of it."

"All my night-things are there," I protested. "I'll need at least my toothbrush."

His voice went cold. "Do as I say, Margaret. Go without it. I'll see you first thing in the morning."

There was that muffled sound again, his speaking to someone. Then he said, "I'll be there around eight-thirty."

I put down the receiver. I'd completely forgotten to tell him about Ellen and 11A Twenty-ninth Street.

I was just sitting there, still staring at the telephone, when Terri returned with a tray of coffee and some sandwiches.

"I didn't know whether you wanted anything to eat, Margaret, but I'm starved. These were left over from a batch cook made earlier for the security men. Did you get through all right?"

I told her I'd had to call Lieutenant Dominic. "He wanted me to tell him when I got back," I said.

Terri laughed. "I bet that wasn't official on his part."

"Nonsense."

"*You* say. You should see the way he looks at you."

I thought, *oh sure*, and said rather stiffly, "Police, whether in a group or single, are one breed that don't interest me."

Perhaps too stiffly. Terri shut up, but not before throwing me that sort of knowing smile people give when they don't believe a word you say.

"He wants me to spend the night someplace other than the Smoke House," I explained. "Because of the telephone."

Terri said that would be no problem, then laughed again. "Maybe Arthur forgot to pay the bill." She sobered instantly. "But, good heavens, you don't know, do you? Of course you don't."

"Know what?"

"About Arthur."

"What about him?" I had the horrifying thought there'd been another murder.

"He's flown the coop."

She told me all about it over coffee. Michael had arrived shortly after I'd left for Front Royal to interview Purcell, only to find the comptroller had left, with two suitcases.

"Nobody has any idea where he's gone," Terri said. "He didn't tell anyone. One moment he was here, the next he wasn't. He cleaned out his desk and his clothes closet and took off. Just like that. Lieutenant Dominic looked fit to be tied, and two hours later a couple of men showed up in a police car and locked themselves in Arthur's office. They were there all day going over the school accounts. But I can't believe Arthur's the one, can you? He's too much of a wimp to have done it."

Half my mind was still on the telephone to Michael, and the woman with him. "Do what?" I asked.

"Murder someone."

I concentrated then on what she'd told me. "No," I said slowly. "No, I agree."

Given Purcell's prior history, his disappearing and the police's looking at the school accounts could only mean one thing: Purcell might well have helped himself to some school money, too. If so, could it be some of the same money Ellen had been getting, and they were in it together? It would certainly seem so, except for one thing. If Patricia Jensen, consultant architect, was a front to hide embezzlement, which I thought had to be the case, why would Purcell have mailed a check to Ellen in Georgetown? Why not just hand it to her in the office?

And why was it that the name Patricia Jensen rang a bell in my mind?

A half hour later, I went to Nancy's room in one of the student dorms. Terri joined me with sheets and a blanket because the bed had been stripped; she had also thoughtfully brought me a new toothbrush. "I had an extra and I didn't want you to have to go all the way down to the Smoke House," she said.

We made the bed and when she left I crawled into it gratefully, feeling almost like a student again.

But sleep didn't come right away. Lying there in the dark, I could only think of "her," the woman in Michael's bed. I imagined she would be tall and slender, and I knew she'd be young and certainly very pretty. I told myself sharply that he had every right in the world to have any woman in his bed he wanted, and I tried to think of George and the years of love and happiness we'd shared. They seemed another life now, though, and loneliness came with its cold hand, as it often did late at night.

Eventually, I drifted off into blessed oblivion, and the next thing I knew it was morning and sunlight was streaming in through the open window.

⁅19⁆

I GUESSED it was about eight o'clock. I rose, used the dorm's bathroom, and dressed in what I'd worn the night before, using what little makeup I carried in my purse to help me face the world.

My stay at Brides Hall had to date been filled with unpleasant surprises, and there were more to come. One was awaiting me right outside the door of the room when I opened it.

She was a short, powerfully built female wearing a too-tight pale-green polyester pantsuit. She had a coarse-boned face with a rather large nose, heavily lacquered hair and gave off a strong odor of stale cigarette smoke. She wore too much makeup, especially lipstick, a good deal of which was smeared over her front teeth. She was in her mid-thirties, I guess. It was hard to tell. I noticed her feet. She wore brown oxfords which could only be described as sensible. There was nothing feminine about her.

In a simpering sort of voice that was unexpectedly reedy and didn't fit her at all, she at once said, "Oh, there we are. Good morning, Mrs. Barlow."

We?

When I just stood and stared, she said, "Officer Burke, Mrs. Barlow, Maryland State Police. Adrienne Burke." A lipstick grin, then, "But you can just call me 'Ade,' most people do. Lieutenant Dominic has assigned me as your bodyguard."

133

I said nothing. I was beyond speech. "Lieutenant Dominic is waiting for you in the dining hall," she said.

I looked her up and down a last time and continued on my way. This had to be some sort of joke. I got out of the building and onto the quadrangle before I realized the awful truth that it wasn't a joke, far from it. She quite literally was dogging my steps. Not immediately behind me, true; she stayed back about twenty feet. But she was following me just the same, step for step. I stopped short.

"I'm sorry, but I don't care to be followed this way."

"Lieutenant Dominic said I was to stay with you at all times."

"Did he now."

It wasn't a question. It was a statement of total incredulity. She wouldn't be there unless he'd ordered her to be, and I simply couldn't believe he would have done this without telling me first. I said nothing more. I turned on my heels and marched across the grass of the quadrangle, heading for Main, resisting a childish impulse to shout back at her, "You have to go around by the path. You're not allowed on the grass."

I was about halfway across when I spotted Michael in the front doorway. When I reached him, I wasted no time in telling him how I felt. "Michael, let me make myself perfectly clear. Whatever your plan is with that creature, I'm not having it."

He was prepared for me—I should have known he would be—and didn't blink. "Creature?" He added a falsely innocent smile.

I waved at the driveway behind me. "You know exactly who I mean. Your police person there, following me around."

His smile increased slightly. "Oh, Officer Burke? She's here to protect you."

"So she told me. And I don't want to be."

He made me wait for what seemed an eternity before he let me have it. Then he said quietly, "What you want or do not want, Margaret, is now entirely irrelevant. If you stay here at Brides Hall, then it's my duty in view of two murders and two threats against you to see you are fully protected. If not responsible to you, I am responsible to the state and people of Maryland to avoid the possible further expense of a third murder investigation. For the same reason, if you refuse protection, I will have to use my authority to escort you from this premise."

It was so unnecessarily formal I almost laughed. Instead, my heart sank because I knew he meant exactly what he said, and the formality was necessary because his job required it. But then, as though nothing untoward had happened, he offered me his usual warmly seductive smile and said, "So that's that. Now let's go have some coffee and talk. I'm sure you have things to tell me."

Without further ado, he took my arm and firmly escorted me into the building. I went submissively.

Officer Ade Burke followed.

My bodyguard sat herself down at a table near Michael and me and had coffee with Curtiss and the six-gun trooper who had that morning resumed his John Wayne law-and-order appearance by wearing his trooper's Stetson. I felt surrounded.

To give Michael credit, he did try. He knew I was upset not just about Officer Burke, but about his playing the heavy police officer. It was hard for me to respond to his abrupt change in mood, though. I felt I was being treated like a child. I realized, however, that I was doing my cause more harm than good by behaving like one. Michael was, after all, investigating two especially brutal murders, and I'd suffered worse than Officer Burke. If she was a new fact in my life, so be it.

He talked about the body bag first. "The ambulance crew brought two to the Repository," he explained. "Don't ask me why. They didn't realize they'd left one behind until the next morning. One man came back, but he couldn't find it or anyone who had seen it. Forensic is down at the guest suite right now going over everything, although I doubt they'll find anything."

Then, obviously trying to spare me any more on that subject, he got onto Arthur Purcell.

"The fraud boys have so far found nothing wrong with any of the school accounts," he told me. "But I suspect, given Purcell's record, that he's engineered something and if so, we'll find it eventually."

I had my moment of triumph and enjoyed it. "Eventually might be too late," I said. "Perhaps I could help."

He looked a little blank, and I promptly produced the furrier's self-addressed postcard and the letter to Patricia Jensen. He looked at both, emitted a low whistle of surprise and then listened silently while I told him about Georgetown and seeing Ellen go into the apartment.

When I'd finished, he was thoughtful a moment, then said, "That's a good piece of work on your part, but don't be too hopeful. The fact that Ellen had keys to the apartment doesn't mean there isn't a Patricia Jensen. She and Ellen could be friends. A good enough reason these days to award someone a contract, it seems. Or she could be a stooge getting paid for the use of her company. But we can check that out."

The moment he started speaking I began to feel vaguely depressed. I'd expected greater enthusiasm. Possibly because I did, I looked past him to Officer Burke. And I suddenly remembered who Patricia Jensen was and why I kept associating her in some way with Brides Hall.

"You don't have to check it out," I said. "She died nearly thirty years ago. She was Ellen Mornay's roommate in Ellen's junior year, when I was a sophomore. She came down with leukemia right after she graduated from college." I added, "And if you want to know what she looked like, turn around."

He did, saw Burke and when he turned back to me, he was smiling. "Well done, Margaret."

I at once felt better, and explained my puzzlement over Purcell's sending Ellen a check through the mail rather than just giving it to her.

"You're right," Michael said. "It could mean a couple of things. It could mean they have no connection in this affair and that Purcell is sending money to someone he thinks is bona fide. Or he's helping Ellen make it look legit by playing it as if it were."

"If that were his game," I protested, "he would have registered the letter as proof it was going to a third party if he were ever asked."

"True," Michael admitted. "Which makes me inclined to think they're not in this mess together."

"Then why would he have run off?" I asked.

"I'm not sure," he replied slowly. "But I suspect because of fear."

"Because even if he's not in it with her, he might be identified with it if she were exposed?"

He looked at me intently and said, "No, I don't think that. I think he ran because he thought he might be the next murder victim."

The distraction of Ellen's apparent dishonesty disappeared. The horror of Mary Hughes and Gertrude Abrams rushed back to take its place, and with it the cold reality that someone at Brides Hall was a killer. The longer I was at the school, I realized, the more difficulty I was having in accepting that fact. Michael must have either read my mind or my expression gave me away, because he said, "You're beginning to have problems with our murderer being here, aren't you?"

"It's hard not to. Michael, are you really certain we shouldn't be looking for an outsider?"

He smiled. "You mean some loony who found an all-girls' school a good place to strike and picked the least likely child to do it to and then came back with police around for the equally unlikely housekeeper? Sorry, Margaret, that sort of criminal would have left clues—they always do. Or would have been seen hanging about. No, we're looking for someone here, I'm sure of it. The kind of person voted most likely to succeed in their high school yearbook. Or most popular. Or best citizen. And ends up cutting the throats of their nearest and dearest while they sleep."

I found myself unexpectedly defensive. "Brides Hall is not an ordinary high school," I insisted.

He laughed. "And old girls stick together?"

I wasn't amused. "That's stupid," I said, realizing he had hit home.

He became serious again. "Is it, Margaret? No matter how much you may have disliked your experience here, you feel something about the place, some sort of nostalgia. Are you certain that whatever that something is hasn't clouded your attitude now?"

"When I first came down here," I replied tartly, "you told me my intimate association with the place could give me an insight no outsider could ever have."

"Yes, I said that," he admitted. "And you've dug up stuff I might never have guessed would be here. But there are two sides to every coin, no?"

There were, I had to agree, and suddenly I felt uncertain of myself and my feelings. I took refuge in bringing us back to Ellen and her apparent embezzlement. "What do you plan to do about Ellen?" I asked.

Michael accepted my retreat with no comment. "Nothing for the moment," he replied. "Let her stew in her own juice for a while. She's got to be pretty uncomfortable. When she started helping herself to Hiram Burgess's money, I hardly think she expected murder and police at school, do you? I could arrest her now, sure, if her trustees pressed charges, but the whole place would be in an uproar and I don't want anything to rock the boat while ferreting out our murderer."

He started to say more but was interrupted by one of his forensic people, who came up to the table and muttered something to him I didn't catch.

"Right," Michael said. He pushed his chair back, bolted

what was left of his coffee, and rose. "Margaret, with your indulgence, I'd like you to look at a couple of pictures with me."

He indicated the door to the dining room and, mystified, I allowed myself to be led away, with Ade, I didn't fail to notice, following.

{20}

MICHAEL DOMINIC'S IDEA OF showing me pictures was to project them on a large twelve-by-ten-foot movie screen in a small viewing theater at the state police forensic laboratories in Baltimore.

His idea of getting me there was by flying me in a state police helicopter which had landed on the playing fields while we were in the dining room.

If anything goes seriously wrong in flight with a helicopter motor or one of its rotor blades, the machine can't fall back on a second motor, or glide, the way most airplanes can. It simply drops like a stone, straight down. Still, despite this, helicopter flight has to be one of the most exhilarating experiences. The way the earth unrolls beneath you if you are flying fairly low; the way you can come to a stop and hover, then descend gently and vertically, has always made me think of a magic-carpet ride.

Our craft was sizable. There were four seats in the passenger compartment behind the pilot, and that meant, of course, room for Officer Burke. I tried hard to ignore her existence, something not easy to do since she sat opposite me and Michael, and although not actually taking up much more of the seat than an ordinary person, seemed to fill the whole plane. We flew quite low, about two hundred and fifty feet by my reckoning. It was too noisy for conversation, so I concentrated as hard as I could on the panorama which unfolded beneath us.

We headed down the Little Choptank River and in no

time at all were out over Chesapeake Bay, dotted every-where with small craft. Once we reached the Bay's western shore, we then turned north up the coastline, over a rolling countryside of greening woodland and tobacco fields until we reached Annapolis, home of the U.S. Naval Academy.

In what seemed just minutes later we had traveled the twenty-five miles and were over the Patapsco River, which led into the busy oceangoing port of Baltimore. We de-scended onto a landing pad in the parking lot of a small office building which housed the labs and took an elevator to the floor where the lab's highly specialized photographic equipment and theater were located. Michael had a tele-phone by his seat and used it to tell the projectionist room to begin. The lights dimmed and suddenly there was one of Mary's photos up on the screen, looking absolutely enor-mous, the wood thrush in the foreground and the blurred figures in the gazebo in the background larger than life.

"Okay," Michael explained to me. "That's a straight print projection from a transparency we made of her negative. It's the clearest of the two shots she took. Now we'll get into specifics." He said, "Next," into his telephone, and a second later the image on the screen abruptly disappeared and a second picture appeared.

This time the wood thrush was gone. Only the back-ground gazebo and the two blurred figures were visible. Seeing them so close made a shiver run through me. It was as though either one might suddenly come alive and step menacingly off the screen into the theater, and I shrank back into my seat.

"This confirms that there were actually two people out there," Michael said. "Both are still unrecognizable, but the one on the left, without the blue jacket, does seem, in our opinion, to be a woman. What do you think?"

I agreed with him. There wasn't anything specific I could put my finger on, no outstanding feminine feature, and the head offered no chance for identification since it was hidden by gazebo woodwork. It was just that the figure seemed feminine and, I thought, familiar. I had no chance to consider why, since Michael said "Next" again into his telephone.

The next picture was such a huge blow-up of just a section of the whole that I almost didn't recognize it. The bottom half of the screen was a blurred blue, the top half a dark-gray mass whose extreme upper part looked nearly black, although I realized after staring at it that the color was actually a deep blue.

"Do you know what you're looking at?" Michael asked me.

I didn't for a moment, but then I realized it had to be the second person. The mass of blurred blue toward the bottom was the blue jacket; the dark-gray mass toward the top probably that person's head. I told Michael so.

He said, "Good. Head of the class. But, as I'm sure you know, the gray doesn't necessarily mean gray hair. It only means deep shadow eclipsed the hair's color. Now, what do you make of what seems a midnight blue?"

"Nothing," I confessed after staring at it a moment longer.

Michael once more picked up his telephone. "Can you give me the outline now?"

What appeared on the big screen now was a progressively lengthening red line. It began in the upper right-hand corner and, following the contour of the deep-blue color, moved left in a gentle arc, suddenly shot straight up and then back down in an arrowhead shape around a very light gray area I hadn't noticed before. It continued to arc gently to the left until, still encircling the blue, it dropped abruptly straight down a ways before turning sharply to the right, heading back aross the screen and rising directly up the side of the blue to the point where it had started.

"What do you see?" Michael asked.

Again I stared for a moment. He waited. The theater was deathly quiet. And then I saw it, and if I'd shivered before, my spine positively chilled this time.

What I saw was a beret, the blue beret with a distinctive

white cockade worn by any crew member of *The Maryland Queen*.

"A crew beret, " I whispered.

I looked at Michael. He nodded. "A blue jacket—our fabric technician says it's suede. Suede always produces a different look than other material on fine-grain blow-ups—no interwoven strands—and a crewman's blue beret. While you were floating about over the Blue Ridge Mountains, we turned the school upside down and found not one but five blue suede jackets. Two were left behind by freshmen and juniors who had gone home; one is owned by Gale Saunders, the *Queen*'s first mate; one belongs to a math teacher who was lecturing here in Baltimore that afternoon, and the last one to a member of the kitchen staff who said it was given to her by a senior three years ago, when the senior graduated. The kitchen-staff lady is sixty-three and fat; we checked on Gale Saunders—she was home in Philadelphia that weekend. My guess is that whoever wore the jacket got rid of it the moment they heard Mary had taken pictures. So let's forget the damned thing."

He sighed, picked up his telephone and was telling the projectionist that would be all when I interrupted.

"Michael, could we see the second picture again? The one with just both figures?"

He said, "Sure," and spoke to the projectionist. The big blow-up disappeared; the second picture took its place. I stared hard at it.

"Michael, the one without the beret, that's Ellen."

There was a moment's dead silence. Then he said, "What makes you say that?"

"I don't know. The way the figure is standing. Leaning slightly. The shoulders. It just looks like her, that's all. Ellen stands like that."

Michael sighed. "So does somebody else, Margaret. Ellen was in New York when this picture was taken. Attending the annual NAPE conference at the Waldorf-Astoria, remember? We checked that out."

I felt a little foolish. "Sorry," I said.

The picture disappeared, the lights came on.

Michael looked at me. "So that's that, Margaret. Why did I want you to see what you just did? I don't really know except I felt it might trigger something for you. I don't quite know what, but something, and that might give us a lead."

He paused, then said, "Blue berets. They're all over the place. Eighteen crewmen and half a dozen stand-ins have them. But who owns the one we just looked at? If we suggest that one of the two people at the gazebo might be our possible murderer, then we're also suggesting it might be the one with the beret, and I don't know, it's hard to put what happened to Gertrude Abrams or Mary Hughes down to a schoolgirl."

To dispute what he'd said, I told him what I thought of Sissy Brown. "For a moment or two when I was talking to her, I thought she was going to get up and attack me."

"I'm not ruling out one of the girls, especially not an athlete like her," Michael said. "The jury's still out on everyone. It's just that at the moment the more likely candidate would seem to be the one you thought looked like Ellen."

I had an odd thought. I remembered Onslow Weekes's wearing Sissy Brown's beret when I'd gone aboard *The Maryland Queen* to question her. "Does Blue Beret have to be a student?" I asked.

"Not necessarily. Who did you have in mind?"

I told him about Weekes, and he made me laugh then, although I felt a touch of chagrin because he always seemed a step ahead of me. By way of answer, he fished a distinctive blue beret out of his pocket, put it on his head and held a hand over his face so I couldn't see who he was. Then he took off the beret.

"I lifted this from Weekes's room when I talked to him yesterday. Our coach having fun at the gazebo with one of the girls and finds out Mary was a witness? That's a pretty straightforward motive, maybe too straightforward."

He pocketed the beret again and rose. "I have to stay

here until after lunch, but the helicopter will run you back now. Forensic will have finished examining your guest suite." He glanced at Ade, two rows behind, then smiled slightly at me. "Officer Burke will be staying in the suite next door to make certain you're not bothered."

I didn't answer. He was bordering on being official again.

He took me back down to the waiting helicopter, saw me and Ade into it, and thanked me for my time. Then, just before the pilot started up the motor, he pulled out his notebook and looked at me intently. "You never told me what you thought of our runaway Purcell," he said. "Your personal opinion of him."

"Voted biggest wimp in his high school yearbook," I replied.

He nodded, deadpan, and wrote in his book: "Purcell. Wimp. Barlow."

And then turned and walked off.

I didn't know whether to laugh, to throw a seat cushion at him, or both. The helicopter motor burst into life and I settled for a fond smile he never saw.

{21}

THAT EVENING I had dinner pretty much by myself, since Ellen was once more staying in Washington, and I had no idea where Michael was, maybe with "her." Terri was working in her office, but took a coffee break and sat with me for a few minutes.

She looked tired out. Parents' weekend was the biggest event of the school year, and preparing for it was endless. Nearly one hundred couples would descend on the school, and there were meals and entertainment to be planned, along with scores of meetings with teachers, the "old-girls' " lacrosse match, and the legendary fathers-daughters mixed-doubles tennis tournament. All the guest suites in the old Smoke House would be occupied, and with Gertrude Abrams gone, there were all the additional housekeeping duties to be supervised.

And, of course, there were the preparations for the big race.

Terri told me she was more than optimistic on Brides Hall's winning. "We've got the best crew ever, Margaret. At least since I've been here. They have a fine edge I haven't seen before."

Listening to her, hearing the excitement in her voice, I found myself involuntarily drawn into a feeling of school spirit and saying inwardly, *And how; we're going to beat St. Hubert's. We're going to sink them.*

We. Us. Brides Hall girls. For a moment, I'd completely forgotten my aversion to the place.

Waiting for the big day, some of the crew were now quartered on *The Maryland Queen* itself, with others sleeping in one of the adjacent boat houses where Curtiss, as a matter of precaution, had posted a round-the-clock security guard. Every morning, released from classes, they hoisted sail and, drifting down Burnham Creek, worked the sixty-foot replica packet schooner out into the Little Choptank. There, they'd usually catch a light early-morning off-shore breeze and would soon be out on the Chesapeake where, practicing coming about or jibbing around a buoy off James Island, the crew cut seconds from the maneuvers.

Leaving Main after dinner that evening, I found myself coming down the steps with Gale Saunders. We exchanged a few polite remarks—I asked her how training was going, she told me "wonderfully." Then, staying with me as I started across the quadrangle, she said quite suddenly, "Mrs. Barlow, you raced on the *Queen* when you were here, didn't you?"

I confessed I had one year.

"Well, why not again?"

Was she just being polite? She was Connie's roommate, after all, and Connie was close to Sissy, who could have less than little use for me. But her lovely amber eyes showed only sincerity.

"It would be fun," I said. "But I couldn't."

"Why not?"

"Rules."

"They changed them some time ago. Each boat is allowed an official observer now."

I laughed. "Gale, thank you, but another adult woman on board, myself in addition to Terri, and I'm afraid your Mr. Weekes would have a nervous breakdown."

Her expression clouded for an instant, and she said sharply, for her, which quite surprised me, "I don't think that would matter."

I didn't pursue it, and by the time she said good night at the Smoke House, she had charmingly persuaded me at least to consider her invitation. "You could time legs for us," she said. "That would be really helpful. Terri is usually too busy below for that. And I'm sure Miss Morney can fix up your official-observer status."

When she'd gone, suspiciously watched after by Ade, I suddenly felt euphoric. Why not board the *Queen* for the race? I was stuck at Brides Hall and it was one of the events I'd really enjoyed as a student. Besides that, I'd be blissfuly free of my shadow for twenty-four hours.

Once in my suite, my euphoria died. I hated the rooms now. The woods pressing in on the rear windows, over which I kept the curtains drawn, the silence of the place in spite of Ade next door, had become oppressive, even claustrophobic.

Far worse was the lingering sense of revulsion I felt over everything that had happened at school. Every corner and aspect of the suite seemed permeated with the horror of Mary Hughes and Gertrude Abrams. Only the bathroom felt safe, and I spent twice as long as usual in the shower. When I finally came out and had dried off, I turned on the television set but soon turned it off again.

I felt a prisoner and started to get ready for bed. What else was there to do but sleep? Reading seemed impossible with the jumble of events from the past ten days filling my mind again, and I began to be overwhelmingly depressed. Here I'd been at Brides Hall, perhaps the very last place I'd ever wanted to find myself, for more than ten days, and hadn't accomplished a thing. I wanted only to go home.

I think I was already in bed, winding up my old traveling clock and setting its alarm, when suddenly something in me rose up in rebellion at being outdone by the dreadful unknown someone who had brought all this to pass. And at the sort of nasty, self-pitying mood I'd let myself sink into. *You're here to help the police discover a murderer*, I told myself, *perhaps even to prevent whoever it is from striking a third time. And to make the place safe for Nancy. So get busy and do something. Anything. No matter how small or ineffectual it might seem.*

But what? I got up and put on my terry-cloth robe and

began to pace. Within five minutes I had seized on something. It was a very small something, but at least it would find me acting and not just sitting around. I immediately felt better. What I thought of was the school log. It might reveal something, no matter how slight, that could prove helpful. What that something might be I couldn't imagine, but I had an absolute compulsion to go and look.

The log was another school tradition. One of the duties of the Head Girl was to keep a written record of every day's important events, just as the captain of a ship daily logs his vessel's progress during the previous twenty-four hours, and any events aboard worth recording. The Brides Hall log was kept on a lectern in the school library on the second floor of Main. No one was allowed to touch it except faculty members, the Head Girl and her Assistant Head. Any infringement of this called for disciplinary action, and sometimes, if the culprit was not popular and the seniors were in a bullying mood, was the excuse for an Inquisition.

One of my character flaws, although occasionally an asset, is impulsiveness. If I get an idea that excites me and I don't act on it at once, I suffer almost unbearable frustration. Over the years, I've learned to temper this impulsiveness by reflecting and weighing the pros and cons, but I admit that such reflection often ends up as a justification of my impulsiveness rather than a brake on it.

Such was the case that night at Brides Hall. My better sense told me to rouse Officer Burke and have her join me. If not that, then wait until morning, when daylight and the usual bustle of school activity would inhibit anyone who might want to harm me. But the impulsive Margaret didn't listen to the common-sense Margaret, and after I put on slacks, a light sweater and my running shoes, and pocketed a small flashlight I always take traveling, I quietly gave Ade the slip and left the Smoke House without her.

The night was silent and, in spite of the quadrangle streetlights and a distant night-light in the front hall of Main, dark, the kind of enveloping darkness that almost seems tangible. There was no moon, and the stars were partially obscured by a thin layer of high cirrostratus clouds which had moved in during the day, the portent of a warm front and probably rain within twenty-four hours.

When the door of my suite had clicked quietly shut behind me, I momentarily got cold feet. It's one thing to decide bravely—or foolishly—in the lighted safety of a luxury suite to cross a nighttime campus where there have been two murders, with the murderer still loose. It's quite a different thing to find yourself actually doing it. I had taken two steps up the path that led from the Smoke House to the quadrangle when I began to feel the way I had the previous night after I'd fled from the body bag: completely vulnerable.

Although the darkness frightened me, I shunned the streetlights to avoid being seen. As I walked across the quadrangle, it suddenly occurred to me that Main might be locked and that I wouldn't be able to get in. Besides feeling vulnerable, I also began to feel a little foolish and almost turned back. But I've never been one to quit something once I've started it, so I went on.

The front door of Main was open, which I remembered it had to be. It never was locked until midnight. This was to allow the Head Girl to come in as late as possible to record in the log any important event that might have occurred during the evening. Despite the security now in effect at the school, someone had decided not to alter that routine.

I don't think there is anything more spooky than a large empty building at night. I quietly closed the door behind me and held my breath for a moment. To my left were the open double doors of Assembly, where the operetta had been given, with its adjoining cloakroom and fateful elevator to the floor above. Ahead was the magnificent broad double stairway, so reminiscent of plantation days, which swept up around both sides of the large open stairwell, first to the surrounding second-floor balcony, now completely dark, then to the third-floor Repository.

Beyond the stairs and down a short corridor were double doors leading to the dining-hall annex and the kitchen, and to my right, the double doors to the study hall, and next to them the corridor down which were to be found the faculty common room, and the administrative offices.

With an uncomfortable sensation that I was being watched, but with the intelletual conviction that I was alone, I headed across the hall for the stairs, reminding myself that I was not an intruder and that I had every right to be there.

${22}$

IT WAS DARK at the top of the stairs. I didn't want to turn on lights that might rouse the curiosity of security guards, so I got out my pocket flashlight and switched it on, beaming it across the large open area of the second-floor hall, which was the same size as the main hall below. At its far end above the front door, two big Palladian windows looked out over the porch roof into the dark night. To the right was the door to the library; to the left, an open corridor leading to the dispensary and the apartments of the school nurse and Gertrude Abrams.

I still felt queasy just thinking about Gertrude. At that moment, wild horses couldn't have dragged me to her rooms. The beam of my flashlight penetrated the corridor only a short way, and as I crossed the hall to the library, I felt as if Gertrude herself might suddenly leap out of the darkness and come after me.

The library was large, endowed by a wealthy alumna with fifty thousand books of every conceivable sort that could ever be needed in secondary education. My flashlight led me past rows of bookcases, reading tables and study alcoves to the log lectern, located near the librarian's desk and the narrow spiral staircase to the Repository.

I switched on a small green-shaded table lamp on the lectern. Shielded from the window by a tall bookcase, I looked around and decided to draw the blinds on the two end windows that faced Burnham Creek and the boat houses. As I started toward them, fear hit me like a blow in the stomach and I gasped. I wasn't alone. Someone was sitting in a chair in a shadowed corner by an index-card file case. I stared, fighting a scream, but somehow managed to make my brain summon up my voice.

"Who's there?"

There was no answer. I repeated my challenge through parched lips. "Who are you?"

Still no answer. Forgetting my flashlight, I came to life, dived for a nearby reading table and turned on another lamp.

And then I saw who it was and the revelation was almost as frightening as not knowing. Leering at me from beneath the protection of his battered hard hat was the familiar face of Dead Monkey.

I took a moment to collect myself, and in that moment, I'm not certain why, I decided to have a look in Dead Monkey's locker, atop the file case. I took it to a reading table, and overcoming my aversion to having any contact with Dead Monkey, reached into the pocket of the horrid thing's back, felt the large tag to which the key was attached and pulled it out. Opening the box, I sat down to have a look.

The thirty-odd baggage tags dated back to 1893, four years after Dead Monkey had made his first unexplained appearance at the school. They were neatly held together with a rubber band, with the one nominating Mary Hughes as the current guardian at the top. The message to her from Vicki Alcott was cruel in its loveless brevity. It was simply, "For Hughes." It must have hurt Mary dreadfully when she put it in the box. She had to have seen the sentimental, sometimes gushy, messages which were written on nearly all the preceding tags: "To Dotsie, the most wonderful freshman ever, with all my love, Anne"; "To darling Anne, with a million kisses and wishes for the best three years possible and luck forever. With tons of love, Emily"; "To Emily, the brightest-ever bride at Brides Hall, I'll never forget you, Penny."

I suppose because of all the needless cruelty and viciousness girls are capable of inflicting on each other in an all-girls' school, my memory flicked back to something that happened when I had been at Brides Hall. I thumbed rapidly back through the cards, looking for one I knew would be just like the one Mary Hughes had received—if Ellen Mornay hadn't thought to remove it.

When I found it, I was amazed she hadn't. The message she as a senior had written in her then bold and unmistakable hand to her freshman was as cruel as the message Mary Hughes had received from Vicki. It was simply, "To Bootsie."

Looking at the fading ink on the yellowing tag brought forth a flood of memories. I saw the campus as it was then, much the same as now, and Ellen Mornay as she was, too, little different in character from today, although, of course, so different in appearance.

And I saw Bootsie, the freshman reject so nicknamed by Ellen because the poor child had a clubfoot. Bootsie had suffered a desperate crush on Ellen, and Ellen coldly had taken advantage of it, frequently getting Bootsie to cover for her when she sneaked off campus at night to meet John Ratygen at the Balustrode gazebo or sometimes in town. Finally, she got Bootsie to fake an invitation from her mother for a weekend at Bootsie's New York home. Since Bootsie's mother was in Europe, Ellen managed to spend each night and most of each day with Ratygen in a Manhattan hotel room. When Ellen graduated and left Brides Hall, Bootsie was stricken and tirelessly wrote her one loving letter after another.

She never received an answer. When she didn't come back for her junior year, news reached the school that she'd gone to Ellen's college to see her. Afterward, when she'd come home, she had thrown herself from a window of her family's apartment.

Remembering that incident now, I began to wonder if Ellen wasn't capable of murder. She'd waited over thirty years to get John Ratygen. With victory finally within her grasp, what would she do if someone threatened to expose her embezzlement of the Hiram Burgess complex money to him? Would she kill? For the first time, I wasn't so sure she wouldn't.

I put the tags back and, trying not to look at the horrible shadowy animal, went to the lectern and opened the large leather-bound log, with a page for every day of the school year. I scanned pages at random and my heart sank. Constance Burgess's entries, in a neat, slightly cramped handwriting, were so extraordinarily brief as to make me think that if I found anything in them at all useful it would be a miracle: "January 9th. School reopened. Mornay's New Year's address." "January 10th. Visit by alumnae, Alice Conway, '58, Mary Bishop, '60, Anne Lloyd-Smith, '60. Met with dorm monitors." The entry for the day of the operetta was particularly concise. "Operetta. Police investigate Abrams's death."

Too concise? Had she avoided saying more for some reason, or was she just lazy? I remembered Terri's comments on her average academic record, which might explain brevity. I also couldn't find any mention of the Inquisition, certainly none of my own meeting with her and Sissy Brown. Mary Hughes's death was only noted once, and then only on the day she was found, and as an "accident."

I had virtually given up when I got to the entry for the Saturday Mary Hughes had trespassed on Balustrode. My eye ran over Connie's cryptic report and my breath caught, literally. She'd written less than ten words, but they were enough: "Next year varsity lacrosse players named. EM/HB lunch Washington."

I slowly exhaled. Perhaps I hadn't come for nothing. EM and HB could only be two people: Ellen Mornay and Hiram Burgess—although Ellen had been in New York that day addressing the annual convention of NAPE. Michael had told me he'd checked that out. Had Connie made a mistake? Or had she been privy to information from her father? I remembered Ellen saying Burgess had flown up to Washington that weekend to lobby some senators about off-shore oil legislation.

In my mind I again saw the shadow figure in the gazebo that I had been so certain was Ellen, and I did some quick mental calculations. Suppose she had made an appearance at the convention first thing in the morning simply in order to be remembered as being there that day, then had slipped away to take the forty-five minute mid-morning flight from New York to Washington. She could have had an early lunch with Burgess, driven out to Brides Hall, a fast two hours away, met with Blue Beret at the gazebo, returned to Washington and been back in New York with just enough time to reappear at the convention and address her associates at dinner. Why, if Blue Beret was someone at school, the meeting couldn't have waited until Monday was something I found a little odd, but I was sure there would be some explanation if I was right in my conjecture.

I didn't get any farther in my musings. I was still staring at the entry when I heard the sound, a kind of scraping, rattling noise, barely audible, but a sound just the same and from within the building.

I stood motionless at the lectern and listened. The only thing I could hear was the faint singing of blood in my own ears. Could it have been Constance Burgess coming in downstairs? There was no entry in today's log and she was due, unless she planned to fill it out tomorrow morning. Head Girls often did, I remembered, and for security reasons she might have been ordered to stay aboard *The Maryland Queen* at night.

I glanced at my watch. It was just past eleven. I went out into the hall, looked down the wide stairwell and saw no one. "Connie?" I called softly.

The sound of my own voice frightened me. If there was someone else in the building, not Constance, it would tell them I was there, too. There was no answer.

Beyond the faintly lit hall, the door to the corridor to Gertrude Abrams's apartment was a black rectangle. Someone could be standing a few feet back from it, watching. I forced myself to call again. "Hello?"

Silence.

Then I heard the sound again. The same scraping rattle, as though a window was being opened someplace, not down the corridor, as I had thought, but up above me. Was it in the Repository? There was a fire escape behind the building. Could someone be trying to get in that way?

I returned to the library and stood quietly by the lectern, listening. I heard nothing.

But I felt something. Barely. At first, I thought it was my imagination. But then I knew it was not. There was a faint draft of cool night air from somewhere. None of the library windows were open. There was only one other possibility. It had to be coming down the narrow spiral staircase leading up to the Repository. That meant the trapdoor at the head of the stairs was open.

What I did next should have earned me the highest possible medal for outright stupidity. I thought I was more clever than a murderer who to date had brutally killed twice and had baffled the police.

I decided to investigate. Deliberately making what I thought were normal sounds of someone who was unaware of anything unusual, I tried to make it seem as if I were leaving the library. I noisily opened and closed the log on the lectern, took two books from a shelf and dropped them on a reading table, turned out the lights, walked to the library door and, remaining in the library, firmly closed the door as though I'd left.

I stood in the darkness, holding my breath. The moon had finally broken feebly through the high cloud layer to shed a faint opaque light through the library windows. As my eyes became used to the darkness, I was able to distinguish reading tables and bookcases; coupled with my memory, this enabled me to make it to the foot of the stairs without banging into anything.

I started up the staircase, careful not to let my running shoes squeak or scuff on the treads. One step, two, three— I was trying hard to breathe silently.

Halfway, I heard another sound. A faint shock, as if someone above me had jarred into a piece of furniture. It seemed to come from someplace fairly distant from the head of the stairs, and that encouraged me. I continued up and reached the top step and stopped again, trying to remember the Repository's layout.

The spiral staircase came out not far from the elevator, which in turn was near the door to the building's main stairway. There was a light switch there, I knew, but between me and it were several rows of steel shelving. Although there was a center aisle to allow passage, what I couldn't remember was how close that aisle was to me. I would have to find the shelving and feel my way along.

Confident I had been completely silent, I reached out and touched the shelving almost at once. Then, careful not to put my foot down on something loose, I started toward what I was certain was the aisle. Once past the rows of shelving, I planned to abandon my silence, flick on my flashlight and make a headlong leap for the door and the light switch.

I never got there.

Moving very slowly, I suddenly felt a strange electric prickling of my skin. All over. Even as I felt it, I knew why. My body had sensed the heat of another body only inches away.

What happened then happened but a second later, even as I realized I had come up against the intruder.

I had no time to react. A hand thrashed at me, grasped my arm and yanked me forward. And my head exploded in a roar of sound and a vortex of purple and red light.

{23}

WHEN YOU'VE BEEN STRUCK DOWN the way I was, with a blow to the head, consciousness returns slowly. Through a haze of confusion, I was first aware that I was in a hospital bed, with the headache of all times. Then I realized that my hips and back hurt; that my right wrist was bandaged and throbbed, and that somebody who had to be a nurse was gently checking on me.

After what seemed a long time, everything became clearer and I recognized Terri Carr seated at my bedside. It was night because a window behind her was dark. Later, I heard her talking to people whom I knew to be a nurse and a doctor. I slept then, and when I awoke my head pounded only half as much and I was able finally to make sense of my surroundings.

Terri was still at my bedside, her expression full of concern. She didn't say much, just told me not to worry about anything. I'd be all right soon, and to rest. But since I've never been able to stand not knowing what there was to know about anything, or to lie quietly for long, I managed to put together enough from my questions and her answers to find out what had happened.

I couldn't remember anything after I decided to go up to the Repository. And she said that of course nobody really knew what had occurred there. But she told me I'd been found on the Repository floor by Constance Burgess, who had come up to Main late to fill out the log. Curtiss had accompanied her from *The Maryland Queen* and was waiting in the downstairs hall until she finished. She was halfway up the stairs to the library when they heard me cry out. There was a tremendous crash, and they rushed up to investigate.

"They found you on the floor with a whole row of steel shelving on you and bleeding from a slashed wrist," Terri said. "Constance made a tourniquet from strips she tore from a costume, and Curtiss called the police and an ambulance, then came and roused me."

By the time Ellen returned from Washington in the morning, the police had a pretty clear picture of the attack. I'd been struck down from behind, like Gertie Abrams, but with a heavy wooden bookend. They found some of my hairs stuck to it. Whoever attacked me had then pushed the shelving down on me while I lay unconscious and had deliberately slashed my wrist with broken glass, figuring to make my death look like an accident. Surprised by Constance, my assailant had dropped the glass too far from me for an accident to be plausible.

Ellen came at once to the hospital to see me. "If not for Connie's quick thinking," she said, "things might have been worse, Margaret."

The shelves were obviously why my back hurt, and Terri told me I was lucky there, too. "The doctor says by all rights you should have crushed vertebrae and a broken pelvis."

I thanked tennis, Jane Fonda and my every-other-day two-mile run.

I had one injury, of course, far worse than anything physical I may have suffered. In spite of what I'd found in the log I had the most awful case of hurt pride. Or should I call it loss of face. Michael arrived at the hospital late in the afternoon, after Ellen and Terri had left. He had an armful of spring flowers and an expression so innocently solicitous that I was immediately suspicious. I let him talk about nothing for a minute or two and then burst out with, "Why don't you stop beating about the bush, Michael, and say it?"

"Say what?"

"What you're thinking. That I haven't played fair with you and that I'm either crazy or stupid or impossible or even all three, because that's what you're thinking, isn't it?"

"Actually, no," he said and gave me that damned smile of his. "Actually, I was thinking how little makeup did for you. You look exactly the same, really, without it."

That left me momentarily speechless, but before I could reply, his smile disappeared and he stared at me intently, almost piercingly. "Okay, Margaret," he said. "You're right. Let's get down to business, and you can start off by telling me what the devil you were doing up in the Repository in the middle of the night."

That put everything immediately back into perspective. I told him how I'd had an odd feeling that I might find something in the school log and had, and then about the draft above and going up to investigate.

He shook his head over my folly. "Do you have any idea who attacked you?" he asked.

I swallowed in frustration. "Of course not."

"Any suspicions?"

"No, except it has to be the person we're looking for."

"Sorry," he replied, "but that's not necessarily a given. There could be two people involved in all of this."

True, I thought. I'd touched on that idea myself. "But where I'm concerned, we can rule out Connie Burgess, at any rate."

"Only thanks to Curtiss."

I was a little taken back by that. "What do you mean?"

"I mean she could have been on her way to Main, seen you, laid a trap and then, for whatever reason, perhaps to deliberately throw us off if she felt we suspected her of Hughes and Abrams, pretended to rescue you."

"Michael, that's paranoid," I said.

He laughed. "I've seen odder things. But that's academic. She has Curtiss as an alibi, unless they're in it together, and to think that would indeed be paranoid. So, yes, we can eliminate Constance regarding the attack on you."

"And Purcell too," I said. "I can't believe he would have sneaked back here to do such a thing."

Michael grinned. "Especially since he was in a lock up. The New York State Police nailed him yesterday afternoon in Syracuse. They're holding him on some minor charges which they may not be able to make stick very long. They phoned this morning to say he claims to have run off because he was terrified he'd be the next victim."

He rose from the chair to fuss with the flowers a nurse had put in a vase. "That's what I thought he'd say," he went on. "But we won't know if I'm right until we get him back here with an extradition order—which might never happen. He lined himself up right away with a very sharp attorney."

He sat down again. "So—the school log. Tell me."

I did. When I had finished, he stared at me for a moment in silence, then whistled. "Very interesting," he said. "Very. We'll check it out discreetly—the airlines, maybe Burgess's secretary. If Constance proves right, I'll want to keep Ellen in the dark about what we know for the time being."

"Why?" I demanded. Remembering Bootsie had made me far less forgiving of Ellen. Coming to see me at the hospital might only have been a clever act to divert my suspicions. "Surely this makes her a prime suspect?" I asked.

He smiled. "Of what? Murder? Or being at the gazebo? Slow down, Margaret. Perhaps you've proved Ellen *could* have been at the gazebo, but you haven't proved she *was*."

"That's her in Mary's photograph, Michael," I insisted stubbornly. "I know it is."

"Sure. But would a court of law agree with you? No face? No distingushing physical feature? Just the way someone stands, the set of her body? And in a blurred, out-of-focus photo?"

I couldn't reply because I knew he was right.

He said, "Look, be patient. It's one thing to suspect, another to prove. To date, forensic hasn't come up with a single clue; not one bit of incriminating fabric, not even one human hair and certainly no fingerprints. Nothing. And until we get evidence, we don't tip our hand about anything we know that could alert the guilty party to cover any traces they might have left uncovered."

Sometimes realism and the truth can seem hopelessly negative. This was one of those times. I suddenly felt over-whelmingly discouraged, as though my whole sortie into the library and Repository had been for nothing. I took refuge in what I'd stumbled onto in Georgetown. "Have you checked out Patricia Jensen yet?"

"Yes, and she's Ellen, all right. The consultancy was in-corporated in Delaware a year ago, with Ellen the sole shareholder and with a Boston address as headquarters— the Washington address is just a mail drop and Ellen's apartment. So far, she's put seventy-three thousand dollars into the company's Boston bank account and has with-drawn sixty-three in cash. We think a good deal of it has gone to pay rent on the apartment—two thousand a month."

Michael hesitated a moment, then said, "Margaret, has it occurred to you that we might not be the only ones to know that?"

It took a second for me to see the point of his question. When I did, I had to wonder why I hadn't asked it myself. "You think someone may be blackmailing Ellen? Blue Beret, notably?"

"It would explain a lot, wouldn't it?"

It certainly would, I agreed.

Michael offered me a conspiratorial smile. "Try this on," he said. "But as an unofficial hypothesis, mind you. Blue Beret demands Ellen cut her or him in on Burgess's money, and along comes little Mary to innocently threaten the golden calf for both. We'd at least have a motive for murder, wouldn't we? For Ellen or Blue Beret."

He was right, but I was so appalled at the callousness of it that it was difficult for me to imagine Ellen risking murder to cover her embezzlement and equally hard to see how a blackmailer would take a similar risk for an even smaller sum of money, since Ellen obviously had already spent most of what she took.

I told Michael this and he shook his head. "The Burgess endowment is worth millions, and a blackmailer could easily demand that Ellen take more. However, and don't ask me to explain why, I have an odd feeling that if blackmail is what is going on, it isn't for money at all."

"What else could it be for?"

"I don't know. We'll see."

"Where do we go from here?" I asked.

"We wait," he said. "Patiently. We try to find the tape, if indeed there was one, or if it hasn't been destroyed, and we hope it turns out to have more on it than just bird songs." He rose to go and then said suddenly, "How do you feel now? I mean about staying on at Brides Hall. Once more, as far as I'm concerned, you're free to go back to New York."

"Which, once more, is what you would like me to do?" I countered.

"As a police officer, of course."

"How about as a non-police officer?" I teased.

He smiled wearily, and I realized then how much of a burden on him I must be. Security considerations for me surely outweighed the value of any further contributions I might be able to make. I knew the best thing would be for me to go and let him pursue the murder inquiry on his own. But I knew I couldn't leave yet. Besides the silent promises I'd made to Sally and Mary Hughes, being on the *Queen* when it raced St. Hubert's had become truly important to me.

I said, "Let's talk about it after the boat race. That's this weekend. I've been invited on the *Queen* as an observer."

He looked slighlty surprised at first, then vaguely amused. "Sort of a last hurrah for the old school tie?"

I hadn't thought of it that way. Was he right? Why indeed had I accepted Gale Saunders's invitation to join the race? And why didn't I want to back out? As Michael himself had said, good or bad, our youth has the irresistible pull of nostalgia. And memory plays tricks, too, tending to make us recall only the good. As an adult, could I finally appreciate what was actually there at Brides Hall and somehow make amends for not seeing it sooner?

I didn't know. I hadn't thought it out yet.

"Call it whatever you like, Michael," I said, "and I'm sorry, truly I am, if I've become a burden."

"I didn't say you had."

"No, but you thought it."

He gave me that totally disarming smile of his, then reached out and ruffled my already rather messy hair as though I were a little girl. "You're not being relieved of Officer Burke, you know."

I think I just stared. "You don't mean you're putting her on the *Queen* with me?"

"Where else?"

"Michael, no!" The sudden spectre of Ade at sea horrified me. "She'll just be in the way," I said.

He shrugged. "She goes or you'll have to stay ashore."

"I am not staying ashore."

"Sorry."

"Michael, you can't do this."

"Yes, I can. And I will."

"The school won't allow it. Saint Hubert's will say we're padding our crew."

He laughed. "I'll have a word with the Saint Hubert's headmaster. And with Mornay."

I saw he meant it and gave up. I wondered if my shadow would get sea sick—we could have some rough weather—and for a moment forgot myself and almost felt sorry for her. "Poor Ade," I said.

⊰[24]⊱

I WAS RELEASED from the hospital three days later and returned to Brides Hall. On the Friday before race day, there
was a final pre-race run on *The Maryland Queen*, and over
Ellen's and Terri's objections, I went along. We cast off
about 9 A.M., coming out of Burnham Creek under power
and catching a light southerly wind on the Little Choptank
which took us under sail on our quarter into Chesapeake
Bay itself. The weather was unseasonably warm and
muggy, and renewed high cirrus clouds told me we might
be in for a few days of rain.

I was comfortably seated on the afterdeck between the
ladder to the saloon and the wheel, keeping a time log of
a series of short legs which put the boat on a different
course. We alternated each change with a jibe or coming-
about, which means changing the boat's course while going
before the wind or into it, respectively.

Ade, of course, was with me, dressed in a powder-blue
track suit, which, because it was a little tight for her, made
her look more like a lady wrestler than ever. She maintained a silent, sour expression, and I had the impression
that she indeed expected to be sick at any moment. I tried
hard to pretend she wasn't there and some of the time
actually succeeded.

I was impressed by the crew's performance, even, I confess, Angela O'Connell's. As ship's message runner, she
took her job seriously and performed well. Gone was the
usual emotionalism of schoolgirls. Under the watchful eyes

of Onslow Weekes and Terri, there was well-disciplined, silent teamwork and instant obedience to the concise commands of their captain, Sissy Brown, who managed both ship and crew with firm and surprisingly quiet authority. She handled the wheel, as did Gale Saunders, her relief, like a veteran yachtsman, with one eye to the huge gaff-rigged mainsail and above it the gaff staysail, as well as to the foresail and jibs beyond, nodding silently from time to time at orders or criticisms from Weekes, who stood close by, watching her and the crew's every move.

By eleven, we had drilled our way through a dozen and a half legs when Terri, taking a break and sitting next to me, pointed off to windward. "Look." A large luxury power yacht, well over a hundred feet in length, was coming down the Chesapeake from the direction of Annapolis. It was a quarter of a mile away, but bearing down on us fast, and I could see a half dozen crewmen in white sailor suits here and there, and a small swarm of passengers on the after sun deck.

"Hiram Burgess," Terri said. "He's had it brought up from Texas for the race every year since Constance began school here."

"Who does he have with him?"

Terri handed me the pair of binoculars hanging around her neck. "He usually invites along a few Texas cronies and favored parents he picks up at Annapolis. He always gives a party for everyone on board after the race. We sometimes have trouble with girls getting drunk at it and getting in trouble with his crewmen or Saint Hubert's boys."

I focused the binoculars. There were at least a dozen middle-aged people at the forward rail training binoculars back on me. They were dressed casually but expensively and looked for the most part as wealthy as the boat they were on. Most had drinks in their hands and a steward with a tray moved among them.

Boats' names are usually always on the stern, and I couldn't see that part of her.

"What's the boat's name?" I asked.

"The *Sam Houston*."

I lowered the binoculars. Boats are feminine and invariably have neuter if not feminine names. "But that's masculine," I said.

Terri laughed. "Tell that to Burgess. He's the one with the gray hair up on the bridge. When he comes up here he likes to show everyone how well he drives. Last year he ran aground in the Little Choptank when he ignored a channel buoy."

I looked again. The *Sam Houston* was closer now, and the binoculars easily picked up the passengers' faces. I had no trouble spotting the Texas billionaire standing at the wheel. He was a big, barrel-chested man with a lionesque head and an overwhelmingly dominating presence. I could see why Constance Burgess might have personal problems. Burgess was the sort of man who never allowed anyone around him even a modicum of self-expression. It was his way or else. Constance might well have stolen in a defiant gesture of self-assertion.

I moved the binoculars back onto the guests and unexpectedly saw a familiar face. John Ratygen. I remembered Ellen telling me he'd be aboard. Then I saw Ellen, too. She was in conversation with four people, away from the rail. She had a drink in her hand and was laughing, head thrown back, as though she hadn't a care in the world. Watching her with the other passengers, I realized how well she had managed to tranform her image into one matching theirs. And I couldn't help thinking of her father, who must have kept up a similar front with society until suddenly it all came to an abrupt and scandalous end. The way, surely, it would end for his daughter now, so many years later.

I gave Terri back her binoculars. "Ellen is up there," I said.

Terri glanced at her watch. "She told me she might be. But she has to be back in school in an hour. Other parents start arriving then."

Thinking of the numbers about to crowd the school buildings and grounds, I was glad to be aboard *The Maryland Queen* and away from it all, even if only for a little while.

"But how will she do that?" I asked, and the question was hardly out of my mouth when I saw how. A small helicopter had appeared from over the Little Choptank and was heading for the *Sam Houston*'s stern, where there was a landing pad.

The yacht was bearing down on us with considerable speed and was now quite close. I was so busy watching the helicopter I didn't realize just how close until I heard Onslow Weeks speak sharply to Sissy Brown. Almost immediately came Sissy's slightly louder than usual command, "Stand by to jibe."

Girls who had been watching the *Sam Houston* suddenly came to life, aware of danger, and leapt for the mainsail and jib winches.

The second command came at once. "Jibe-ho."

We were on a starboard tack, sailing on our quarter. Sissy spun the wheel, the *Queen*'s bow fell rapidly off as she swung downwind. Winch handles whipped around, close-hauling the mainsail and foresail booms to lessen their throw across the deck when, with the wind behind us, the boat would swing sharply over onto a port tack.

When it happened, it happened quickly. One moment we were heeled slightly over, the next we leveled in the water and the booms of both main- and foresails, the mainsail one massive, began to swing head-height across the deck toward the opposite side.

"Heads down." That was Sissy shouting at Ade, who stood like a zombie in the path of the mainsail boom. One girl leapt from her winch and tackled her to the deck. The mainsail boom, moving fast enough to crush a skull, missed the fool woman's head by an inch.

Up on the bow, the main jib's boom cracked across the deck like a whip. Anyone standing in its path would have been overboard in a flash.

The *Queen* shuddered from the shock of the heavy mainsail block coming up short on its traveler rail; we heeled over slightly and instantly gained way again.

I don't think the *Sam Houston* missed us by more than fifteen yards. As the huge form went rapidly past us, there were shouts of "Go *Queen*" and "Go Brides Hall," and I caught a glimpse of laughing, oblivious-to-disaster passengers and the gray mane of Hiram Burgess on the bridge as he Texas-whooped a greeting to his daughter. Any normal skipper of any normal sailing craft would have lodged a complaint with the Coast Guard. But *The Maryland Queen* was not an ordinary sailing boat, nor her crew ordinary yachtsmen. The boat and her crew belonged to a school which was beholden to the owner of the *Sam Houston* for millions.

When we were left rolling in its wake, I glanced at Sissy Brown. She wore a faint smile and was looking at Connie Burgess, who, clearly embarrassed, pretended to be coiling rope.

Terri was white. And furious. "If he'd hit us," she muttered between clenched teeth, "guess who would have had her career ruined. If not killed with everyone else."

She was right. I had no problem imagining headlines that would somehow shift the blame for a disastrous accident from a billionaire, influence-peddling oilman to an Assistant Headmistress and a sailing coach. If the *Queen* had not swung off sharply and jibed, the big power yacht would have plowed right through her, and three or four girls below decks would almost certainly have drowned.

We docked an hour and a half later, sails furled, deck secured and coming up Burnham Creek under power. Ellen, with a large group of parents, some with their daughters in tow, was on hand to greet us.

I left the boat after turning over my time log to Terri and was trapped into exchanging a few pleasantries with Ellen. I found it hard to keep up pretenses. Knowing that she was a thief and soon would be arrested for embezzlement, to say nothing of her being a murder suspect, made it difficult for me even to look at her.

"Margaret, you're extraordinary," she said warmly for the benefit of the parents with her. "Yesterday," she explained to them, "she was still in the hospital from a whole row of steel shelves falling on her."

Or pushed by you? I wondered.

I escaped as soon as common courtesy allowed and, dogged by Officer Burke, headed across the playing fields. I was nearly to the other side when I heard my name called, and I turned. It was Constance, who'd run from the *Queen* to catch up to me.

She caught her breath and said, "I'm so sorry about that near miss with Daddy's boat."

"It was hardly your fault," I said.

"Daddy's impossible. He thinks the *Houston*'s a little runabout." Then, in a rush, she said, "Mrs. Barlow, would it be possible to talk with you a moment?" And staring very pointedly at Officer Burke, added, "Privately?"

"Of course," I said. "Now?"

"If you have just a few minutes, yes, please. In my room? No one else is there."

Neither of us spoke until we'd reached the senior dorm. I insisted Ade remain out of hearing range a few feet down the hall from Connie's privileged corner room.

We went in. Connie closed the door behind us and locked it. "Please sit down, Mrs. Barlow."

I had a moment when I thought, *My God, suppose Michael is right and her rescuing me was simply to throw us off and Curtiss was in it with her.* But then I got hold of myself andpulled up her desk chair. She was clearly very nervous about something, twisting one hand in the other, but finally she said, "I have something which could be important. I mean, about Mary Hughes and Gertrude."

She stopped. I waited. "Maybe it's nothing at all," she went on. "It's a tape I found. I think it must be the one Mary made."

·{25}·

I MANAGED TO KEEP my voice calm. Just. "Why me, Connie?" I asked. "Shouldn't you hand it over to Lieutenant Dominic?"

Her eyes became guarded and she almost stammered her answer. "Well, I thought they'd think it funny I was the one who discovered it. I mean, you know how the police can get. I . . . well, I wanted to make certain before I got involved with a lot of questions from people who didn't know anything about the school that it really was important."

I realized that what actually bothered her was her previous experience with the police. But I wasn't there to condemn; besides, I owed her one.

"I understand," I said. "Tell me where you found it and how."

She looked relieved. "It was after you'd gone off in the ambulance. I went to the library to do my school log. I mean, I was there in Main, wasn't I, and it had to be done. Anyway, I saw the key to Dead Monkey's locker on a reading table and went to put it away, and when I put it in his pocket I felt something at the very bottom. It was a cassette. I took it with me and played it. There's nothing on it but some bird songs and some voices you can hardly hear."

Nothing but bird songs and voices! I stared hard at her. Was she innocent of the implication in what she said? I had to believe she was, and that she wasn't covering up

172

that she'd had the tape all along and was getting rid of it this way for fear of getting caught with it.

With a certain chagrin, I realized I must have just barely missed finding it myself. "Do you have any idea how it got there?" I asked.

"No. None at all."

"Why do you think it might be important?"

"Because it wasn't there when we got Dead Monkey back from the police and I brought him up to the library. So that means someone put it there since then. And I heard the police were looking everywhere for a tape after Gertie died. Curtiss told me that. Do you want to hear it?"

I told her I did, and she got it out of her bureau drawer and put it into her cassette player. I held my breath in expectation and at the same time dreaded what I might hear. Whatever was there could be the reason for two murders.

It was obvious that Mary had turned on the recorder almost as soon as she entered the Balustrode woods and then had simply left it on. There was the haunting call of a cuckoo, a long silence before another call. During that silence I heard the muffled sound of an aircraft passing overhead. There were vague noises I could not really identify, perhaps Mary moving or fussing with her camera. There was a metallic sound, as though she had bumped the recorder against something, the cuckoo again and then the clear warble of a wood thrush. There was another long silence and another aircraft. By now I was thoroughly disappointed, and had just about written off the tape as worthless when I suddenly heard the voices. Or was it just one? I wasn't sure, but it was definitely a woman's voice raised in anger.

I strained to hear. The voice seemed far off, indistinct, and was interrupted by the wood thrush again, then some metallic sounds. Finally I did hear a second voice, just a confused murmur behind the first voice, but I was certain of it. Both voices continued for perhaps thirty seconds, then suddenly the tape was dead silent.

"That's all," Connie said. "I don't know why it would have been put in Dead Monkey. Except to hide it there in a hurry until a better place could be found."

That was the only reason I could think of, too. When Connie took the cassette from her player and handed it to me, I found holding it very strange. It was almost as though the tape had life. Mary Hughes's life. And perhaps the life of the person who had murdered her. I felt both presences strongly, almost physically. I think Connie did, too. Her expression was an odd mixture of fear and awe.

You may be right," I said. "This could be important. It's going to need a sound expert, though."

"A sound expert? Why?" Connie looked blank and then she said, "Oh, no, Mrs. Barlow. The voices?"

I nodded.

"You mean Mary might have heard something she wasn't supposed to. And one of those voices found it out and . . ." Her eyes were wide. "I never thought of that. I . . ." She broke off, her hands to her mouth.

A sudden sharp rap on the door made us both jump. "Mrs. Barlow?"

It was Officer Burke deciding she'd been out of earshot and contact long enough.

"Coming," I said.

I put the tape in my bag.

Connie lowered her voice. "Will you have to tell the police that I was the one who found it?" she asked. She looked desperately anxious.

"It doesn't pay to lie to them, Connie," I answered. "It always comes back to haunt you. But would it help if I twisted arms a little? Lieutenant Dominic told me he's been in touch with the Ft. Worth police about the trouble you were involved in there. But I'm sure he can be made to see it's really no concern of his."

She turned scarlet and then looked grateful. "Would you, Mrs. Barlow?"

I laughed. "Depend on it."

I rose from her desk chair and went to the door. She

went with me and suddenly grasped my arm. "Oh, wait a minute," she cried, "I almost forgot." She went quickly to her desk and brought back a photo album. "Remember this? You dropped it on the floor of the Repository."

"Me?"

"Didn't you?"

I took the album, opened and recognized it immediately. It was one of a set of thirty covering the school, its student body and their activities since Brides Hall was founded. A quick glance showed me its subject matter was Brides Hall sailing, going back to 1910 and emphasizing the annual race with St. Hubert's beginning in 1934.

I didn't try to figure out why Connie thought I'd taken it upstairs with me. Instinct told me that I might have more evidence on my hands and I didn't need to explain that to her. I said quickly, "Of course. I had forgotten. Thank you, Connie."

She came downstairs with me and we parted, she to go back to the playing fields to await her father's helicopter arrival, I, dogged by Ade, to return to my Smoke House suite and prepare for the buffet-lunch reception for parents at Main in an hour's time. I crossed the quadrangle and the album burned under my arm. I tried to think why it had been in the Repository. It didn't make sense that a student would have taken it up to that gloomy place where murder had occurred just to look at pictures. But it made sense if the murderer had taken it to dispose of it, and accidentally dropped it.

But when? When I was attacked? When else? That would mean the murderer was in Main and was in the act of taking the album or had already taken it and perhaps was even hiding the tape, too, when I interrupted.

The thought that all the time I was coming up the main stairs, entering the library, studying the log and Dead Monkey's tags, someone who had killed two people was only a few yards away, setting a trap for me, made me chilled with fear.

But why? Why was the album important in the first

place? Perhaps, I thought, somewhere in it was a clue to the murderer's identity.

In my room, safe for the moment from Ade and everyone else, I fixed myself a drink and settled into a chair with the album. I began to study it, page by page, picture by picture, beginning with old, faded photos of long outdated sailing boats, the single-masted skipjack "draggers" which until only a few years ago had plied the shoals of the Chesapeake, bringing up oysters by the ton. Time had changed the boats and the clothes the girls wore, along with the fashions sported by spectator parents, but nothing had changed the type of person distinctly represented in every girl's face. In any group photograph, whether in 1928 or 1988, there is no difficulty in identifying the bully, the clown, the non-entity, the troublemaker, or the one girl among all of the rest who seems adult.

An hour later, when I'd finally reached the last page and had closed the album, I put in a call to Michael Dominic. I didn't have proof positive, but I had begun to have a horrified conviction that I had finally seen the face of the murderer.

{26}

WHEN I CALLED the station house, I was told Michael was out. I left a message asking him to return my call as soon as possible, changed clothes for lunch and then I tried to think of what to do with my evidence.

I didn't dare leave the album lying about; I could hardly bring it with me the way I could the tape. It had to be hidden someplace. But where? I thought of Officer Burke's room next door and decided that if there was to be another unwanted visit to the Smoke House by the murderer, Ade's quarters as well as my own would be searched.

Finally, I settled on the toilet. I shut off the water, flushed it, enclosed the album in a plastic bag to protect it against any lingering dampness, and put it in the now empty tank. Then, with Mary's tape securely in my handbag and shadowed by Ade, who was wearing a ghastly floral print too painful to describe, I went to the buffet reception.

The dining room, the downstairs hall and Assembly were crowded with parents and their daughters as well as alumnae of all years, and I managed without difficulty to duck Ellen Mornay and thus any further comments she might make about my recent "accident." I found myself cornered, however, by several old classmates, grandparents like myself, who seemed astonished to find me there. I hardly recognized them. No amount of expensive clothes could ever disguise downright dowdiness, nor an air of having long ago given up on life.

"We haven't seen you in years, Margaret. Where on earth have you been?"

I refrained from saying "Living," and managed to find socially acceptable excuses for my absence from alumnae functions. I also managed to act and sound as much like an overgrown preppie as my interrogators.

I was brought up short in my intolerance when I ran into several others I'd known at school who were of quite a different nature. These had done a wonderful job with their lives. One was a medical research scientist; a second had an excellent record in Wisconsin politics and now was that state's Lieutenant Governor; a third had achieved considerable distinction as a sculptress. Schools such as Brides Hall may turn out a full measure of vacuous socialite women who expend remarkable amounts of energy in life not doing much of anything except being "volunteers" in one socially acceptable project or another—for "acceptable," read non-controversial—but nearly all also turn out a responsible handful of extraordinary people.

After lunch, I went back to my suite. My telephone message light was dark, indicating that Michael hadn't called me back. Waiting for him, I made the fatal mistake of lying on the bed and promptly falling asleep. When he finally did call, I awoke not knowing at first where I was and fumbled about seemingly forever before I managed to locate the telephone and pick up the receiver.

"Hello?"

"You called."

Called whom? When? Had I? And why? As consciousness slowly returned, I began to remember. "Yes," I said. "Yes, I did. I've got the tape."

"Ah? I'd better come and get it then." His tone was completely off-hand. No excitement in his voice at all. And he didn't say anything further, ask me how I'd come by it, anything like that. Feeling rather let down, I told him I had something else, too.

"Oh? What?"

But I didn't say. I'd decided that what I'd discovered in

the album needed to be seen to be understood. That was part of it. Mostly, though, I was just plain irritated by his casual attitude, and childishly told myself he could wait to find out until I was good and ready to tell him.

I said, "It will keep until I see you."

He didn't challenge that. "I'll meet you in half an hour then."

"Where?"

A moment's silence before he said, "The chapel. Use the vestry door. I'll unlock it for you."

The chapel had been under police seal since Mary's death, with vesper and Sunday services being conducted in Assembly. I hated the thought of going into the place and protested. "Why on earth the chapel?"

"If I'm right, there are a million parents there today and Mornay playing hostess. Correct?"

"Yes, but—"

"I'm not anxious for her to see me talking to you, and the chapel is the one place she won't be going."

"She could see us going in."

"She can't see the vestry door from Main and she won't question my being there if she sees me."

"What about Ade?"

"Who?"

"Officer Burke."

"She can wait for you in the Smoke House. I'll call her."

Thus it was a half hour later I found myself leaving the Smoke House guest suite with Mary's tape. But only with the tape. If Michael were to agree with what I was certain I had discovered in the album, I knew he would never let me board *The Maryland Queen*, and that was something I was determined to do. So I did not bring the album nor did I intend to mention it to him yet.

Nothing had ever prepared me for that strange musty odor most churches have. When I closed the vestry door behind me, it enveloped me like a cloak, more so than usual because the chapel had been shut up for two weeks.

The vestry was a small room, nothing more, really, than

a cloakroom with a bare table, chairs and an oak cupboard in which were kept extra prayer books and a teapot, along with cups and saucers, although why the latter were there I could never understand. I'm certain generations of students came and went without ever using them.

The door from the vestry into the chapel proper was open and the chapel gloomy in spite of bright daylight sifting through its stained-glass windows. Gloomy and damp. And deathly silent, a silence so isolated and complete that anything which broke it from within was bound to frighten.

I told myself not to be foolish, and went in. All I could think of at that moment was death and Mary Hughes. The place seemed filled with the horror of what had happened to her. I got as far as the first row of pews when there was a sudden sound from up in the balcony. I nearly jumped out of my skin.

"I'm up here."

I looked up, and through the murkiness saw Michael leaning on the balcony rail looking down at me.

Being in the chapel was bad enough. The thought of being where Mary had died was too much. "I'm not going up there," I said.

"I'll come down." And he disappeared into the balcony's darkness. A moment later he was by my side.

"We might as well sit right here," he said.

I obeyed, and we sat in pews across from each other. I produced the tape from my handbag and gave it to him. "There are maybe ten minutes of tape before the wood thrush," I said, "and it's not until then that you can hear voices. They're very faint."

"You can't tell whose?"

"No. I wasn't even certain at first if there were two people or one."

He turned the tape over once or twice, eyes fixed on it. I couldn't tell what he was thinking. Finally, he glanced up at the balcony and slipped it into his pocket. "We'll put the electronics boys to work," he said. He smiled for the first time. "I taped Mornay a couple of days ago when she didn't realize it. So we'll do a voice print on both voices and see if either matches, and if Mornay's does, it will prove once and for all that she was at the gazebo."

I thought about the second person, Blue Beret, whom I was certain I'd seen in the album. "What about the other one?" I asked.

"Unless they call each other by name we might have to voice-print the whole school to get a match there, which we can do, of course, but it will take time."

Forever, I thought. *And what I've seen in the album could perhaps do the same in days.*

Even as I was thinking that, I heard Michael say, "What's the other thing you had?"

I'd hoped he'd forgotten.

Although everyone we suspected except Ellen would be on the boat during the race, and I could virtually be staking myself out like a lamb to snare a wolf, I refused to let Michael persuade me not to go—which he would have done if I'd told him about the album. In a way I almost welcomed a face-to-face confrontation with the murderer. If that was to happen on the *Queen,* so be it. This time, I didn't plan to be caught in the dark, unable to identify my assailant. I knew who it would be, I was certain, and would be on my guard.

I answered Michael as blandly as possible. "There was nothing, really, just an idea."

Not bland enough. He looked at me suspiciously. "An idea about what?"

"It was just a silly thought. I'd rather not say."

He didn't accept that either. "You're not leveling with me, Margaret."

"I don't know what you mean."

"Yes, you do. You're holding something back."

My smile, I hoped, was completely guileless. "Michael, we're partners, not competitors. At least I hope so."

The look he gave me was long and searching. I think he

knew I was lying. But if the sound boys couldn't come up with positive identification, then staking myself out might be our last chance.

Michael suddenly looked at his watch. "Okay, time for your silly boat practice."

"It's sail inspection on shore," I said. "We have to check the canvas for weakness or repair."

"Whatever," he said. "And you're already five minutes late."

I didn't ask him how he knew that. I mutttered something about good luck with the tape and I'd see him after the race.

Ten minutes later, I was on my hands and knees on the lower playing fields next to the wharf along with Terri, Onslow Weekes, Sissy and Gale Saunders, inspecting inch-by-inch the vast yellow/white surfaces of sail, jibs and stay-sails. They were spread out on the grass, and regardless of murder, as I worked I began to feel the excitement of the upcoming race.

·{27}·

RACE DAY, I was due at the school kitchen in Main at eight o'clock to help Terri with last-minute inventory provisions. I had no trouble getting up. Ade saw to that. At seven, she unceremoniously began pounding on my door.

"Mrs. Barlow?"

I staggered to the connecting door between our two suites and there she was, all dressed in her powder-blue tracksuit and ready to go.

"Ah, there we are. We wanted to be early, didn't we?"

The "we" and being spoken to as though I were a child told me that she'd been conferring with Michael and put on the qui vive. That meant I was going to be shepherded and shadowed as never before. I silently thanked my lucky stars we'd be on a boat where she would be out of her element and heavily restricted.

"Thank you," I said, and promptly closed the door.

Fifteen minutes later, showered, made up and zipped comfortably into my faded yellow flight suit, I headed for Main, with Ade right behind me.

I couldn't face a dining hall which, at that hour, would still be filled with parents and their daughters. I went around Main to the service entrance to the kitchen.

The kitchen was a beehive of activity and I didn't see Terri. One of the harried cooks told me unpleasantly, "She's in there," and waved a huge knife in the direction of a side pantry. I found Terri and two senior crewmen, smart in their royal-blue sweatshirts and -pants and their distinctive blue crewmen's berets with the white cockades. Everything that would be eaten on board the *Queen* during the next twenty-four hours, as well as a few extras, was laid out on two long pantry counters. We checked off each item against Terri's inventory, deciding to abandon one or two things and to add a few others in their place. When we had finished, the two girls loaded everything into boxes and those onto two large dollies, which they wheeled out to the service door and the school utility van, which would drive them and the supplies down to the wharf.

Ade, who had managed to coax an enormous plate of eggs and bacon from a cook, was obliged to abandon it half-eaten when Terri and I hurriedly finished cups of coffee and unceremoniously departed.

Outside Main, the school grounds were dotted everywhere with parents and their daughters heading for the *Queen* to see off the packet schooner and her crew. We avoided them wherever it wasn't too apparent we were doing so. For some reason, most parents of children in boarding school, perhaps more than those with children in public school, seem convinced that any teacher has all day to talk to them. We were in too much of a hurry for that.

As we crossed the playing fields and neared the *Queen*, I could see the *Sam Houston* anchored in deep water in the Little Choptank. A hundred yards away was a smaller yacht which had joined her.

That was the Committee Boat, an old-fashioned, spacious veteran with a large saloon and an oversized bar, chartered each year for the race. Loaded with parents and alumnae from both Brides Hall and St. Hubert's as well as a number of society columnists, it would accompany the race until sometime around dusk, returning to anchor for a parents' dinner given by both schools, this year at St. Hubert's. The next day, Sunday, it would cruise down the bay again to meet the two schooners and accompany them back to the finish line.

A third boat, a thirty-six-foot cabin cruiser, would accompany the competitors all the way from start to finish. This was the Chase Boat. It was specially equipped with first-aid and rescue equipment and had on board a paramedic, two professional frogmen and a high-speed outboard-powered rubber raft which could be launched in seconds. It had been a standard fixture of every race for seventeen years, since *The Maryland Queen* had been dismasted in a violent middle-of-the-night squall. One girl with a broken leg was transferred to a passing fishing boat, but two others who had been swept overboard were in the water for nearly two hours before they were finally picked up by the Coast Guard.

By the time Terri and I reached the wharf, it was ten o'clock. I saw Ellen, looking smart in an expensive linen suit. She was talking to Hiram Burgess and John Ratygen and to a woman I recognized as a television personality.

The launch from the *Sam Houston* had come wharfside to take them, along with other selected guests, out to the yacht. A larger, slightly less luxurious yacht was approaching to ferry those who would board the Committee Boat.

I was about to step onto the gangplank to follow Terri on board when I felt a tug at my sleeve. It was Ade, looking more out of place than ever. "Mrs. Barlow? I'd like a word with you, if you don't mind." It wasn't a request, it was an order.

"What is it, officer?"

"In private, ma'am, please. We'll just step over there a moment." She nodded at the school van, emptied of its cargo of provisions and parked unattended away from the crowd.

This is it, I thought. *Michael's put one over on me. I'm going to be officially stopped from boarding the* Queen.

I went meekly with Ade to the van, and when she nodded at the front seat, dutifully got into it.

She got in beside me, looked about to make certain we were neither seen nor heard and then said, "Lieutenant Dominic told me I'm not to let you board the school boat unless you carry this." She opened her shoulder bag and produced a small automatic pistol, a .28 Beretta, I learned later, which she extended to me butt-first.

I stared at it, astonished. "What makes you think I know how to use it?"

"The Lieutenant says you do. It's loaded and on safety."

I looked and saw it was. I only had to slip the safety catch and pull the trigger. I smiled inwardly that Michael had researched me the way he had everyone else at school. Obviously he'd learned that my husband had bought me a licensed handgun when we'd lived on a relatively isolated ranch near Santa Fe, New Mexico, where he had worked for a year.

It was on my tongue to say "I don't want it," but I didn't. For once I thought twice. It was illegal for Michael to arm me unofficially this way; he could even be risking his job and police career by doing so. The gun told me two things: Michael's concern for me, and his confidence that I wouldn't use the weapon irresponsibly.

After a moment of silence, I took the automatic and dropped it into one of the deep padded leg pockets of my flight suit. The padding was thick enough to disguise the shape of the gun.

"Anything else?" I asked.

"That's it," Ade said and favored me with a wide grin. I found myself staring at the lipstick on her teeth. Sometimes little things like that stand out at such moments.

"Well, let's go then," I said, and got out of the van, with her following me. We were just in time. We'd just boarded when Sissy Brown blew two short blasts on a whistle and summoned her crew off the wharf and to their stations.

Two of the eighteen-girl crew were stationed at the main and foremast halyard winchs; two at the mainsail and foresail sheets; one at the jib halyards; two at the jib sheet winches; one at the heavily geared centerboard winch just aft of the main mast.

With Sissy Brown at the helm, that made nine assigned stations. Of the remaining ten girls, eight lined the rail, wharfside, and two were on the wharf itself, unsnubbing spring and hawser lines to cast the boat off. Once out on the Bay, they would go below to await their watch. Until 8 P.M., the watch would change every two hours. The rules, established over the years, prohibited anyone off-watch to assist in sailing the boat except in the case of someone overboard or the boat's becoming disabled. This was to prevent numerical superiority being used to overcome deficiency in training and performance. With nothing to do on deck, crew members off-watch invariably went below for much-needed rest and to eat or warm up.

I was due below to help Terri in the galley, but I delayed going down in order to see us get underway. Sissy quietly ordered both sails raised along with the main jib, and when they were, called out, "Back the main jib" and ordered the mainsail and foresail sheet winches to be slackened off. A faint breeze in Burnham Creek rippled the surface of the brown, bracken water. When the backed jib had filled and swung our bow slowly away from the wharf, both our sails caught the wind and we got underway with the cheers of everyone on shore mingling with the throaty roars of the *Sam Houston*'s horn and the shriller sound of the horn on the Committee Boat.

The mood on the spectator vessels was so festive it was hard to believe that the school buildings in the background had only days before been the scene of two awful murders. It was as though Mary Hughes and Gertrude Abrams had either been forgotten or simply been dismissed as unimportant.

But not by everyone. A fourth boat had appeared unobtrusively to tag after us at a discreet distance. It was low and black and not much larger than the *Sam Houston*'s launch, but it had a small cabin and looked built to take any sort of weather. I recognized what it was at once. It was a police boat.

⟮28⟯

TERRI AND GALE SAUNDERS were in the fo'c'sle, a narrow cabin space forward of the galley which conventionally serves as the sleeping quarters of a boat's crew. When underway it was a rough place for rest. Even though a crewman off-watch was so tired that any place to stretch out was a gift from heaven, the pounding a boat took in rough or choppy weather was always far worse up in the bow.

On *The Maryland Queen,* the fo'c'sle doubled as a sail locker, and besides the eight bunks there were four large open bins where extra sails and jibs were neatly stowed in big blue nylon bags clearly stenciled as to the contents. One of the bunks had been assigned to me, and Terri had another directly opposite. Six others would be occupied by girls off-watch, with three other girls sleeping aft in the saloon.

Terri and Gale were making up my bunk and they laughed when I protested their doing my job. We'd gathered way by now and the *Queen* had begun to heel over as we pointed close-hauled into the wind. Terri braced herself against the bunk as she went on tucking in a blanket. "Relax, Margaret," she said. "You've already pulled your weight a thousand times."

She started to say something else, but her eyes suddenly shifted to the fo'c'sle doorway behind me. "She's in here, officer. No need to worry."

I half-turned. Ade stood in the doorway. I simply stared. I didn't have to say anything, events took care of that for me. Our bow suddenly dived into the choppy wake of some passing powerboat and Ade, clinging to the fo'c'sle bulkhead, turned positively green right before our eyes.

Gale said pleasantly, "You'd feel better, officer, if you stayed above."

Ade glowered, started to reply, then, turning greener still, gave up and fled.

Gale laughed. "She's really a troll, Mrs. Barlow. I saw her hustle you into the van on the wharf. How can you stand her?"

The automatic Dominic had forced on me suddenly felt heavy in the leg pocket of my flight suit. "She means well," I said charitably.

I helped Terri and Gale make up their bunks, then Terri and I went to the galley to finish putting away the provisions. It took us the better part of forty minutes, and during that time we moved out of the Little Choptank River into Chesapeake Bay itself.

I could tell from the motion of the boat that the wind had freshened considerably. We were well heeled over on a starboard tack, and rose and fell on long swells which meant a strong southerly wind coming up the Bay. I put on a sweater and over it a crewman's light nylon sou'wester that would shed both wind and water. When I went up on deck to my observer position just forward of the mainmast, I was glad of my foresight. All sense of onrushing summer was dispelled by the wind and the occasional cold spray which lashed our decks whenever we hit a heavier than usual wave. I felt that wonderful exhilaration experienced by anyone who loves the sea and sailing: the thrill of hurtling forward drawn by some tremendous invisible power, the beautiful sight of taut canvas overhead which seems to fill the sky; the bowstring tension of rigging, the hiss of water foaming past the hull, the wonderful tangy saltiness of the air.

We were close to James Island now, and for the first time in many years I saw our sister ship and arch-rival, *The*

Chesapeake. She was reaching on the same tack as we and only a hundred yards off to windward. I had brought up binoculars along with the chronometer and clipboard I would use to time legs during the watches I would alternate with Terri, and I focused in. The well-drilled crew of young men wearing bright-red yachting sweat suits were at their stations. After I had been watching them for a few seconds, their helmsman, a tall, muscular young Viking with a shock of unruly blond hair, gave the order to come about. As her crew moved with impressive machinelike precision, *The Chesapeake*'s bow swung up, her mainsail and gaff staysail, then her foresail and jibs, cracking and thundering as she gained way.

I heard Sissy cry out to "Stand by to come about," and then give the order to do so. We came about ourselves, now directly astern of *The Chesapeake.* If Sissy could outpoint the other boat without losing speed from being too close-hauled, we had a chance to beat them to the red buoy off the north end of James Island, which marked one end of our starting line; the Committee Boat, three hundred yards beyond, was at the other end. I could just make out the buoy, a dark stub of a stick which, when I trained the binoculars on it, materialized into a bright-red pointed can projecting above the water about six feet and looking for all the world like a huge artillery shell.

I had timed our change of tack. From the moment Sissy called out "Hard-alee," to the complete refilling of our main jib, seven seconds had elapsed. I noted it on my clipboard and then kept an eye on *The Chesapeake* to see what she would do next. I didn't have to wait long, perhaps two minutes. *The Chesapeake* skipper decided to put himself upwind from *The Maryland Queen* before she did it to him, and came about smartly. I was watching the young Viking and saw him bawl out "Stand by" to his crew. The next time he opened his mouth, I pressed the start button of my chronometer, stopping it the moment *The Chesapeake*'s main jib refilled. Six seconds. We'd have to do better.

I mentally guessed it would be fifteen seconds before Sissy brought us about again. I was close. Twelve seconds after *The Chesapeake* changed tack, we did, in six seconds this time, in spite of the fact that Ade once more nearly got herself knocked overboard by the mainsail boom and had to be shouted to her knees.

My watch said eleven-forty. A moment after I'd checked it, Onslow Weekes gave a sharp blast on his whistle and spoke for the first time. "Twenty minutes."

We were close enough to the Committee Boat to distinguish faces. Sissy brought us about just as I spotted a woman I could have sworn I'd roomed with for a year—I never did find out—and, with the wind coming up the Bay almost perpendicularly across the starting line, we made a leisurely heading on our quarter back toward the red buoy three hundred yards away.

Our rival, now on an opposite tack, was heading for the Committee Boat. I began to feel a surge of intense excitement, which I tried to control by telling myself that in a race that wouldn't finish until tomorrow noon at best, it really didn't make much difference which boat gained a few seconds on the other by crossing the starting line first.

During the following fifteen minutes, we jockeyed for position, with Weekes giving a minute-by-minute countdown.

When the starting cannon boomed from the bridge deck of the Committee Boat and the black "start" pennant shot up its halyard to the boat's stubby masthead, we were close-hauled on a starboard tack only a few points off the wind and moving at full speed. I was sure we would be over the line before time. If so, we'd have to swing around and go over again, possibly losing minutes to *The Chesapeake*, and something more important than time to our crew's morale—prestige.

But we didn't fault. Photographs later showed us only one second short of doing so, half a bow's length perhaps. We were clipping along at twelve knots, our lee rail well under water, and we beat *The Chesapeake* across by a full boat length. I glanced back at Sissy Brown. She was absolutely relaxed, her powerful hands firm but easy on the helm, face expressionless as she eyed her mainsail luff-line, looking for any telltale belly in the canvas that would show her she was too close to the wind. I've almost never seen anyone under pressure look so calm and poised.

There were nearly sixty miles of choppy Chesapeake Bay water between us and our return buoy off Tangier Island far to the Southeast. With the wind also from the southeast we would have to beat our way into it down-bay, tacking endlessly back and forth across the Chesapeake, which, around Tangier Island, was nearly thirty miles wide. The weather bureau had predicted rain, as I had guessed from my own observation of the lowering cirrostratus cloud layer. And that night, some heavy wind. There was a great deal of traffic in the Chesapeake: oceangoing ships headed for Baltimore; private power and sailboats going anywhere and everywhere. We were in for a long, wet and watchful afternoon and night.

I settled down to enjoy the first phase of the race and the fact that we'd started off in the lead, no matter how slight. But when I saw the low black hull of the police launch dogging us some five hundred yards off to our windward, my good feeling fled. It forcibly reminded me of the danger I was in, and once again the automatic in my flight-suit pocket felt hideously present and leaden.

When Terri appeared through the galley hatch with a mug of steaming hot coffee for me, everything I felt must have shown on my face. "Margaret, are you all right?" she immediately asked, an anxious look on her face.

"Yes, I'm fine."

"Sure?"

"Sure."

"If it helps, Officer Burke just lost her breakfast in one of the heads."

I laughed and took the coffee and said I was just feeling

a little let down after all the pressure and excitement of the start. She blew me a kiss and dropped back below. I couldn't tell her the thoughts that had been in my mind. There was nobody on board I could confide them to except Ade, and I wasn't about to discuss anything with her. In spite of every resolve, I felt unbearably vulnerable.

⁖{29}⁖

HALFWAY THROUGH the first watch that afternoon, the wind really picked up. Whitecaps appeared on the water and our beat south brought a lot more spray over the decks. From time to time we also got a heavy dousing as the *Queen* buried her bow in a wave and a wall of water swept over the decks. Sissy Brown drove her hard. She was one of those intensely competitive people who simply must win, and she was determined to get everything out of her schooner that the boat had to offer. Not only was she clearly determined to avoid reefing unless absolutely necessary, but in a near-reefing wind she was carrying staysails and all three jibs as well as full sails. Sometimes we were heeled over so far that our entire lee rail was under water.

There was plenty to be done. I helped Terri serve lunch and afterward made fast a number of things in the saloon that kept banging about. On watch, I stayed at my station with my clipboard and chronometer, the latter now in a plastic bag to keep it dry, and taken out only when I had to make notations.

The afternoon passed rapidly, and soon we had completed the second watch. Twilight fell and we got our first taste of rain, which made visibility difficult. Both Sissy Brown and Gale Saunders, her first mate who spelled her on watches and with the navigation, had their hands full with dead reckoning. It's not easy to keep a boat, under sail in rough weather, on course and make points on time and with accuracy. There are so many variables: wind direction and force, tide, the boat's speed forward and slippage—the boat's drift to leeward. Although confident in the girls' training and ability, I was comforted, just the same, by the knowledge that Weekes was monitoring our progress in the control cabin.

Trouble, which had lurked with us from the moment I boarded, finally materialized at ten o'clock in the evening.

We were midway through the first four-hour watch. We had lost sight of *The Chesapeake* as darkness fell. Like us, she wore running and masthead lights and had been about a half mile to leeward when I last saw her. It had also been some time since I'd seen any of the boats following us, including the police launch.

I was in the navigation section of the saloon, portside of the massive centerboard well, watching Gale Saunders plot our next leg when Sissy, on deck at the helm, brought us sharply about from a starboard to a port tack. The *Queen*, which had been heeled well over, swung up level, pounded its bow into the heavy seas for a second or two, then rapidly heeled over on her other side as we got underway again. A second later, there was a heavy thump on the deck overhead, a sharp cry, and we swung back into the wind, luffing, our main and foresails thundering. Obviously something unexpected had happened.

I threw on my sou'wester and hurried up, Gale right behind me. Weekes and Terri were already there.

After the lights of the saloon, even though they were always dimmed to make adjustment to the darkness on deck easier, it still seemed pitch-black topside. Compared to the calm below, the strong wind, the sails thundering, rain sheeting across us and the boat wallowing and pitching, seemed violent and dangerous.

The crew carried waterproof flashlights when on watch. The one in Weekes's hand shed a sharp white beam, silhouetting four shadowy forms surrounding it who were bent low to avoid the mainsail boom which danced inches above their heads. The light picked out the shiny chrome surface of the big mainsail winch. Weekes reached down and his rain-wet hand spun the handle freely. The winch mechanism had broken, releasing the mainsail sheets and letting the huge mainsail fly free.

The mainsail on a Chesapeake Bay packet schooner is big, nearly six hundred square feet of canvas; the boom is eight inches in diameter, over twenty-five feet long and very heavy. It usually took three of the crew, using everything they had, to lift its stern end onto the boom crotch when furling sail. Although the sheet was double-blocked, the pull on it, especially with the sail wet and sailing close-hauled, was far too heavy for one girl.

For what seemed an eternity but was probably only a few seconds, nobody spoke or moved. Everyone just stared. I suppose we were all just taking in what had happened. Vicki Alcott, the school heavyweight, came to her senses first. She grabbed the flying main sheet, pulled it taut against its block on the fantail traveler rail and, putting her back to it, pulled the boom most of the way in, then snubbed the sheet on a cleat and made it fast. The *Queen*'s bow fell off, mainsail and foresail filling again, and we started to get underway once more.

"Can you close-haul more, Vicki?" Sissy asked.

"You'll have to luff up again, skipper. And I'll need help."

Both the regular mainsail-winch crewman and I stepped forward. Terri stopped us. "Wait a minute," she said. "This needs muscle." She beamed her flashlight around and stopped on the familiar face, minus lipstick, of Officer Burke, of all people, who had roused herself from "dying" of seasickness and followed me up from the saloon. Terri grabbed her arm. "Here," she commanded, "get hold of that rope." She propelled Ade across the deck to Vicki.

Ade was used to orders and she laid her big hands on the sheet. As Sissy spun her helm once more, we slowly came back up into the wind, the tension easing off the sail as we luffed. "Now! Heave!" Vicki shouted. And she and Ade hauled in on the sheet. The boom came in steadily, the sail tightened.

Sissy shouted, "That's good."

Vicki had just made fast the line when one of the winch crew on the forward deck yelled back, "Fouled jib!"

"Oh, God," Terri cried. "Hold her up, Sissy." And she headed forward at once, flashlight winking into the driving rain.

Without thinking, I stumbled up the heaving deck to help.

It was the main jib that had fouled, the only jib that carried a boom, and it was the boom end that had caught up in a loose pennant halyard. This in turn had snarled around the starboard foremast stays, adding to a confused jumble of wet rope. Getting out my own flashlight, I could see Terri stretching up with a boat hook trying to free it. But the jib was a big spread of canvas, and as Sissy still held us in a luff, the jerking and tugging of the boom end of the jib made her task nearly impossible.

It was a job for hands, not a boat hook. Both winch crewmen had stayed at their stations, ready to winch in the sheet as fast as they could when it was freed. I wrapped a leg around the stay to keep from going overboard and stood with the other leg up on the gunwale, stretching to unsnarl the lines. It seemed to take forever. Twice I was up to my waist in water, and trying to hold my flashlight on the tangle while untangling it at the same time made the job even more difficult. But I finally succeeded, the boom end came free to lash back and forth across the deck.

I heard Terri shout, "Winch in" and her shout saved me because it snapped my attention back to her instead of to the deck where I groped for a footing as I came down off the gunwale.

I heard her shout. I turned. I saw the winch crew, back to me and to her, spinning their winch handles. I swung the light onto Terri. I saw her face just before she swung the boat hook at my head. A horrible, twisted, savage face contorted with rage.

There wasn't time to duck. The long shaft of the boat

hook caught me across the forearm as I lifted my hand defensively. The pain was shattering. My hand went numb, my flashlight went flying.

No one can think at a time like that, only react. I let go of the stays, collapsed on the deck and tried to get my good hand into my flight-suit pocket for the automatic. She struck a second time then, just a dark shadow looming over me, and the only thing that saved me was the *Queen*. The winch crewmen had close-hauled the jib, Sissy had spun her wheel to bring the boat off a luff, and the wind immediately heeled the *Queen* over hard.

Caught off-balance by the suddenly slanting deck, Terri missed my head. I took the blow on my shoulder. It hurt but I finally freed the gun, though I never got to use it. My fingers were numb from unsnarling the tangled ropes, and as I fumbled to release the safety catch, she leapt on me and yanked it from my hand.

At that instant *The Maryland Queen* dug her bow into a heavy wave. A wall of solid sea water smashed two feet deep over the foredeck, and Terri, failing to brace herself against it, went crashing with me across the deck and up against the starboard gunwale.

The force of the fall nearly stunned me. When I pushed to my knees I saw that Terri was face-down under me, a dark inert form in the scuppers. I heard a shout. A light flashed on us and then, as the *Queen* dug her bow fully under a second time, I was lifted up by another solid wall of pummeling water. I felt a terrible jar as I smacked into a stay, and the next thing I knew I was overboard, as was Terri, our bodies tumbling and rolling against each other.

I had a brief vision of a light near the helm and silhouetted figures, then everything was inky, wet darkness.

For the second time I owed my life to a Brides Hall girl, this time Sissy Brown. She saw us go over the side, instantly brought the *Queen* up hard, at the same time shouting, "Crew overboard." If she hadn't been so alert and quick I would have been lost.

It was a call for all hands on deck. The crew reacted fast.

Seconds later, two self-inflating life rafts, stowed port and starboard, hit the water, each with an identification light and radar screen. Two stern searchlights were sweeping back and forth over the water. I saw them but they didn't see me. I had already gone too far astern. *The Maryland Queen*, although only a few hundred feet off, looked a mile away to me.

Because of the *Queen*'s lights, the other alerted searchlight found me first, the one in the bow of the police launch. The launch pulled aside within a minute; I couldn't have lasted much longer. Keeping my head above water and Terri's, too, with one arm useless and weighed down by sodden clothing, was not something I could do for long.

Hands grabbed at both of us. Everything was confusion; wet and darkness and pain, bone-chilling cold and men's voices. And then I was down in the launch's small cabin, huddled on a settee wrapped in blankets, with two huge troopers staring down at me and Michael Dominic pushing a mug of scalding tea into my good hand.

"Can you tell us what happened?" he asked gently.

I did not speak right away. I was looking at Terri, on her back on the settee opposite me, her eyes closed and blood from the back of her head soaking the blanket beneath her. She looked innocently asleep, her face especially pretty in the soft cabin light.

"She died moments after we pulled her from the water," Michael told me. "A fractured skull. She must have hit her head going overboard."

I remembered the terrible wall of sea sweeping over the deck and smashing Terri and me down into the gunwale. And the look on her face before that as she swung the boat hook. "She tried to kill me," I said.

I couldn't say more. I thought of the group pictures in the album I'd studied showing Terri, in a blue suede jacket and crewman's blue beret, smiling out from among the various recent crews of *The Maryland Queen*. Terri in a blue suede jacket and crewman's blue beret. Terri, who, I had begun to realize, was the person who could have a motive and be anywhere on the school grounds because she had the right to be.

I heard Michael say, "You knew it was her, didn't you? That's what you were going to tell me, damn stubborn fool, and decided not to."

I didn't answer right then. I couldn't. I'd been right and I didn't want to be. I think I'd prayed she wouldn't be the murderer. Even now, looking at her, I wanted so desperately for her to be innocent; to be the lovely young Terri, so filled with life and energy.

But she wasn't innocent. She'd cold-bloodedly killed two people and she had twice tried to kill me.

{30}

I HAD TO ENDURE another stay in the Cambridge hospital. I was flown there by police helicopter, this time to have a cast put on a fractured right forearm and to be treated for shock. Before the helicopter arrived, Sissy Brown came aboard the police launch, pushing past a bewildered and shamefaced Ade.

"You were super, Mrs. Barlow," Sissy said. "And listen, we're going to win this damned race, okay? You can count on it. We're going to win it for you."

Impulsively, she bent and squeezed my good hand. As for me, disliking her as I did, I think I've cared for few people as much as I cared for her at that particular moment.

The *Queen* did win, coming across the finish line at James Island nearly a mile ahead of *The Chesapeake*. It had been decided not to cancel the post-race party on board the *Sam Houston*. Parents, friends and crews were still at it when I returned around seven in the evening from the hospital. The doctors didn't want me to leave for another day and raised the devil when I released myself, but I'd had enough.

I didn't join the partying, however; I couldn't. The memory of Mary Hughes and Gertrude Abrams, of Terri Carr, and the knowledge of Ellen Mornay's ruined life were too overwhelming for me to feel anything but a deep and wrenching sadness. I went to my Smoke House guest suite and to bed.

I spent much of the next day and evening with Michael adding things up and, at one point, making an official statement about my own role since I'd come down to Brides Hall. It turned out that the voices on Mary Hughes's tape were indeed Terri's and Ellen's. Enough of what they said was revealed by the wizardry of modern sound engineers to allow Michael Dominic to confront Ellen and, later, Arthur Purcell. Ellen, knowing Purcell's background, had seduced him into covering and aiding her embezzlement with promises of a share in the take. Once involved, his guilt guaranteed his silence.

What Ellen took was not a large sum compared to the overall endowment, only slightly more than a hundred thousand dollars. But it was enough to pay for all that she considered vital for her success in her last chance to catch John Ratygen: the rent on the "love nest" in Georgetown, plastic surgery, a smart sports car, and a wardrobe of fashionable new clothes.

She would have succeeded except for one person: Angela O'Connell. From the tape and Ellen's confession, the girl's role became all too clear. She had hardly been at school a month when she discovered she could step off a path into concealing bushes directly beneath Ellen's office window. When the weather was fair and the window open, she could eavesdrop to her heart's content. Seeking to curry favor from Terri, she'd reported a talk between Ellen and Purcell which revealed what they were up to. Terri easily bought Angela's silence with threats of an Inquisition by seniors. A few nights spent poring over the school accounts when Purcell was away confirmed for Terri the truth of what Angela had said she'd heard.

Everyone has his or her particular dream of life's ultimate prize. For most, the reward remains elusive, and they resign themselves to never achieving it. For a very few, however, failure is unacceptable, the dream too magnetic. Obsessed, they will risk everything to realize it—even murder.

I've thought a lot about Terri Carr and the dreams of an underprivileged child from a depressed area of West Virginia. Had she always seen herself as Headmistress one day of a famous preparatory school? Or had she seized on this only when she first came to Brides Hall and saw in Ellen Mornay a similar and never secret ambition? We would never know, although I suspect the latter. On that fateful Balustrode Saturday when Hiram Burgess telephoned the school to order Ellen to lunch with him in Washington, Terri immediately contacted Ellen at the Waldorf-Astoria to relay the message and triumphantly reveal what she knew. Then, reveling in her power, she'd forced Ellen into a confrontation at the gazebo that very same afternoon.

As Michael had guessed, her demand had nothing to do with money. Terri wanted Brides Hall. Ellen was to retire at the end of the year with a guarantee from the trustees that Terri would have her job.

Her dream within her grasp, Terri could take no chances on Mary Hughes's being a possible witness to her blackmail. Nor on Gertrude Abrams's. Whether she murdered Gertrude because she feared the housekeeper might have identified her on the tape, or whether she thought Mary might have confided in Gertrude was something that would never be known.

To avoid further scandal and also believing they probably couldn't find anyone able to match the job Ellen had done, the trustees decided not to press charges against her and to keep her on as Headmistress. She had to pay back what she'd taken, of course. The money was to be withheld from her salary over the coming years at a rate that would quickly return her appearance to one of dowdy middle age. And John Ratygen was lost to her for a second and final time. I could not help but feel a little sorry for her.

As for me, I could finally go home and the following day after breakfast I packed up. Michael provided a trooper to drive me to New York, and I left the old Smoke House with the trooper carrying my luggage and cameras. At Main, looking about me, a funny thing happened. I suddenly didn't want to go. My old station wagon seemed a stranger, and I realized with surprised shock that I was apprehensive of the real world to which I would soon be returning.

I watched the trooper put my baggage into the back seat,

telling myself I was being childishly emotional and I had to pull myself together. *You're not a schoolgirl any more, Margaret. Go home,* my head said.

No, I wasn't a schoolgirl and hadn't been for a long time. But just the same, something in me cried out to stay a little longer. I had an intense feeling of lonely nostalgia, although I'm not really sure for what. For Brides Hall and my own student days? For what had been and was no longer? For lost youth? I suspect a little of each. I asked the trooper to wait, and I walked slowly across the playing fields to the wharf and boat houses. And as I walked, I remembered: the long winters of classes and study-hall periods; room-mates liked and disliked; teachers, some dull, some hateful, some loving. I remembered school rituals and traditions familiar even now; friends made, laughter and tears shared; victory and defeat on the playing fields. And I remembered the shrill exhortation of schoolgirl spectators when I won the interschool tennis championship to bring the cup back to Brides Hall after an absence of twenty-six years.

I walked and looked around me and let myself accept the past. I wouldn't come back, I was certain of that. Not even for Nancy. From now on that had to be her mother's responsibility, not mine. But I knew, in spite of everything, that the Brides Hall in me was something I could not and should not ever again separate from the rest of my life the way I had always tried to do. In a strange way I loved the place.

The Maryland Queen was tied up, silent, sails furled, every rope neatly coiled and in place, the decks scrubbed, the brightwork polished. In the stillness surrounding me, it seemed impossible to believe what had happened on board her only thirty-six hours before.

I thought of Dead Monkey, two weeks ago—it seemed a lifetime, at least—hanging a few feet over the deck, and I shivered, not in horror of the shabby creature, but with the thought of how close everything at the school had come to being brought down like a house of cards. Brides Hall would go on as always—for Nancy, probably for her daughter if she had one, for generations more of young women. But how fragile everything in life is and how dangerous to regard anything as permanent.

I was still there ten minutes later, staring blankly at the water, when I became aware of Michael Dominic standing beside me. He'd walked up silently. He glanced at my arm, in a cast and a sling, and asked if I was okay, and I said yes.

The sound of distant laughter and someone singing the school song drifted up the quiet waters of Burnham Creek from the *Sam Houston.*

"They're celebrating," I said.

"They can. None of them were really involved."

"And any danger is over?"

"The out-of-the-ordinary kind, yes."

I watched a loon flying low out over Burnham Creek, dark wings rising and falling slowly, rhythmically, like a heart beating. Watched and in my sadness felt a deep gratitude for life.

He said suddenly, "It's no, isn't it?"

He meant himself and me. I looked at him. His dark hair was tousled, he was in profile, face averted, as though not daring to see refusal in my eyes, his chiseled features strong. I recalled how I'd first seen him standing in the chapel door. He was one of the most attractive men I'd ever met.

"I'm sorry, Michael."

I didn't say more. I didn't think I needed to. I felt he knew why not, that it might have been save for the experience we'd shared. The horror of that prohibited it for me.

He smiled faintly and took my hand. "May I ask again, sometime?"

"I hope you do," I said. "A lady always likes to have the prerogative of changing her mind."

I reached up and kissed him hard, and then walked quickly back across the playing fields. Half an hour later, the Chesapeake was behind me and I was heading home.